Rascal

DOES NOT DREAM

of a

Nightingale

HAJIME
KAMOSHIDA

Illustration by
KEJI MIZOGUCHI

Sakuta Azusagawa

Still doesn't own a smartphone, now a college freshman. Managed to get into the same school as Mai, and they're enjoying their time together.

Rio Futaba

Freshman at a national university. Was nearly always in the science lab in high school, but it sounds like she's made some friends at college. Works part-time at the same cram school as Sakuta.

"Lemme take one.
Let's call it *Arrival at Enoshima*."

Yuuma Kunimi

One of Sakuta's few friends from his time at Minegahara High. Entered the workforce after graduation—which first meant six months of training. Now working as a firefighter.

"Now I sound like the bad guy!"

Mai stuck out her lower lip, then took a sip from the mug in her hands.

"You put in too much. It's really bitter."

Mai Sakurajima

A famous actress, her career is back in full swing. Going to college with her boyfriend, Sakuta. Between work and classes, she's very busy, but treasures the time she spends with him.

She was standing by the windows, near the front row.

Her street clothes looked out of place in the classroom.

Bathed in the light of the setting sun, the sea breeze played with her hair.

Ikumi Akagi

Sakuta's classmate back in junior high.
In the nursing program at Sakuta's university.
A dedicated student, she founded a
volunteer group, but lately, her attentions
have lain elsewhere…

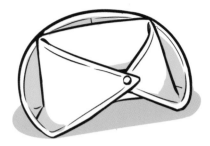

Rascal
DOES NOT DREAM
of a
Nightingale

HAJIME KAMOSHIDA

Illustration by
KEJI MIZOGUCHI

New York

Rascal Does Not Dream of a Nightingale
Hajime Kamoshida

Translation by Andrew Cunningham
Cover art by Keji Mizoguchi

This book is a work of fiction. Names, characters, places, and incidents are the product of the author's imagination or are used fictitiously. Any resemblance to actual events, locales, or persons, living or dead, is coincidental.

SEISHUN BUTA YARO WA NIGHTINGALE NO YUME WO MINAI Vol. 11
©Hajime Kamoshida 2020
Edited by Dengeki Bunko
First published in Japan in 2020 by KADOKAWA CORPORATION, Tokyo. English translation rights arranged with KADOKAWA CORPORATION, Tokyo through TUTTLE-MORI AGENCY, INC., Tokyo.

English translation © 2023 by Yen Press, LLC

Yen On
150 West 30th Street, 19th Floor
New York, NY 10001

Visit us at yenpress.com
facebook.com/yenpress
twitter.com/yenpress
yenpress.tumblr.com
instagram.com/yenpress

First Yen On Edition: June 2023
Edited by Yen On Editorial: Ivan Liang
Designed by Yen Press Design: Andy Swist

Yen On is an imprint of Yen Press, LLC.
The Yen On name and logo are trademarks of Yen Press, LLC.

The publisher is not responsible for websites (or their content) that are not owned by the publisher.

Library of Congress Cataloging-in-Publication Data
Names: Kamoshida, Hajime, 1978– author. | Mizoguchi, Keji, illustrator.
Title: Rascal does not dream of bunny girl senpai / Hajime Kamoshida ; illustration by Keji Mizoguchi.
Other titles: Seishun buta yarō. English
Description: New York, NY : Yen On, 2020. |
Contents: v. 1. Rascal does not dream of bunny girl senpai —
v. 2. Rascal does not dream of petite devil kohai —
v. 3. Rascal does not dream of logical witch —
v. 4. Rascal does not dream of siscon idol —
v. 5. Rascal does not dream of a sister home alone —
v. 6. Rascal does not dream of a dreaming girl —
v. 7. Rascal does not dream of his first love —
v. 8. Rascal does not dream of a sister venturing out —
v. 9. Rascal does not dream of a knapsack kid —
v. 10. Rascal does not dream of a lost singer —
v. 11. Rascal does not dream of a nightingale —
Identifiers: LCCN 2020004455 | ISBN 9781975399351 (v. 1 ; trade paperback) |
ISBN 9781975312541 (v. 2 ; trade paperback) | ISBN 9781975312565 (v. 3 ; trade paperback) |
ISBN 9781975312589 (v. 4 ; trade paperback) | ISBN 9781975312602 (v. 5 ; trade paperback) |
ISBN 9781975312626 (v. 6 ; trade paperback) | ISBN 9781975312640 (v. 7 ; trade paperback) |
ISBN 9781975312664 (v. 8 ; trade paperback) | ISBN 9781975312688 (v. 9 ; trade paperback) |
ISBN 9781975318512 (v. 10 ; trade paperback) | ISBN 9781975343507 (v. 11 ; trade paperback)
Subjects: CYAC: Fantasy.
Classification: LCC PZ7.1.K218 Ras 2020 | DDC [Fic]—dc23
LC record available at https://lccn.loc.gov/2020004455

ISBNs: 978-1-9753-4350-7 (paperback)
978-1-9753-4351-4 (ebook)

10 9 8 7 6 5 4 3 2 1

LSC-C

Printed in the United States of America

Not here
Not here
Not here I cried
Over and over and over again
Searching for anything good about me
Finding only things wrong about me
I'm right here
In a world I loathe
Hoping for love

From Touko Kirishima's "Hilbert Space"

Chapter
1
Heroism

1

Sakuta Azusagawa was meeting friends outside the gates of Katase-Enoshima Station.

It was the last Sunday in October, the thirtieth, and the time was just before noon.

The sky above was beautifully clear, the sunlight warm.

Perfect day for an outing.

The recently remodeled station elegantly welcomed throngs of tourists to the ocean's depths. A striking arched gate, elaborate decorations, and tanks of jellyfish supplied by the new Enoshima Aquarium—these fixtures made it seem even more like the fabled Dragon Palace.

Next to Sakuta, Yuuma Kunimi was muttering, "This place sure has changed." Sakuta thought Yuuma had changed far more dramatically.

Back from six months of firefighter training, Yuuma had noticeably bulked up. Even when he was fully dressed, it was clear how ripped those arms and chest were. He'd cut his hair short, and even his face in profile looked way more grown-up than the last time they'd met.

Was that what happened once you entered the workforce?

Firefighters save lives, and maybe that responsibility fostered a new-found maturity.

The time they'd been apart had made him positively virile.

"Kunimi," Sakuta said, his tone the same as it had been in every one of their high school conversations.

"Mm?" Yuuma glanced his way.

"Do you like miniskirt Santas?"

"I wouldn't say that."

He didn't even sound curious. His eyes went right back to the station building.

"Then do you *love* them?"

"Absolutely." Yuuma nodded for emphasis.

He might look like he'd grown up, but he was still willing to play along with the dumbest jokes.

"If an attractive miniskirt Santa came strolling along here, what would you do?"

"I'd do a double take."

"Same."

"Then stare *real* hard."

"Mm-hmm."

The banter came as naturally as breathing, and they both laughed— until a new voice interrupted.

"How long is this degeneracy gonna last?"

Sakuta and Yuuma both spun around.

The last to arrive—Rio Futaba, looking thoroughly disgusted.

She wore a loose-fitting basic tunic and slacks that stopped just above her ankles. On her feet were a pair of casual short boots, which must have had rather thick soles—she seemed taller than usual. Lately, she'd been wearing contacts, but today she was back to her glasses.

But why did she show up behind them instead of coming through the station gates?

Before Sakuta could ask, she shrugged. "I got here early, so I walked around a bit."

"It's been too long, Futaba."

"Same, Kunimi."

"Let's catch up once we sit down. The shop'll be packed by noon," Sakuta said.

They headed toward the water.

"Sakuta, Futaba. You've both changed a lot since we last saw each other."

Yuuma glanced from one to the other over his boiled whitebait bowl.

They were at a popular seafood restaurant by the tourism center a five-minute walk from Katase-Enoshima Station—if you caught a green light on Route 134, only two or three minutes. They'd arrived before noon but found it already teeming with customers.

A glance around suggested the crowd was mostly tourists here to see Enoshima. Many were grabbing a bite before they crossed the bridge or otherwise taking a break on the way back.

"How have *I* changed?" Sakuta asked. He didn't think he had. The only obvious difference was that he'd graduated and was no longer in his Minegahara uniform.

"You're the one who's become a whole new person, Kunimi," Rio said. She was sitting next to him, eating the staff special, a bowl of rice topped with *namero*—seasoned minced fish. This came covered in a large sheet of seaweed, which made it possible to roll your own sushi. You could then pour the soup over the leftovers, *ochazuke*-style. The dish offered different flavors and textures as the meal progressed, which made it a popular choice.

"How have *I* changed?" Yuuma asked, just as confused as Sakuta. Maybe humans aren't conscious of their own transformations. You see yourself every day but never notice the little changes adding up.

"Your hair, your face, your build—they're all different now," Rio said.

"I guess?" Yuuma said, sounding like he understood what she meant but also didn't.

"How's the firefighter life treating you?"

Sakuta was aware that firefighters existed and had an idea where the local fire stations were, but he was surprisingly fuzzy on what their actual job entailed.

"We alternate twenty-four-hour shifts with off-duty days. Like, this week I started yesterday morning and was at the station until the same time this morning. Then the next squad came to relieve us, and now I've got the whole day off. Tomorrow morning I'll be back at work, taking over for them."

"And on the clock until the next morning?"

"Yep."

That sounded pretty rough, but Yuuma didn't seem to think it was a big deal. If he was struggling, it didn't show.

"So you came straight here after working all night? Aren't you tired?"

"We take turns napping! In uniform so we can roll out at a moment's notice."

"Huh. But I guess if you're alternating like that, you get a good amount of time off."

That's what it seemed like to Sakuta, considering that half the time would be spent outside of work.

"But off duty doesn't mean a day off," Rio pointed out.

"Futaba's right. If I get the call, I've gotta head straight in. And since I'll be on a long shift again tomorrow, I'm supposed to rest up so I'm good and ready."

"Resting is part of the job, then?"

You definitely wouldn't want firefighters partying so hard they couldn't do their jobs.

"Basically, yeah."

It was a fairly unusual career, quite different from the relaxing college life.

"You're all professional and shit."

"That's right—I've got a *real* job. Pays so good I can order a rice bowl *and karaage.*"

For emphasis, Yuuma grabbed a piece of chicken off the plate and tossed it in his mouth. He seemed to be savoring every bite. By high school income standards, that was the height of luxury. They would've never even considered meeting at a restaurant this pricey back then.

"Bourgeois scum," Sakuta said, swiping some chicken for himself.

"You can have some, too, Futaba."

"Just the one," she said, showing far more restraint. She even went out of her way to pick the *smallest* piece. Was that because Yuuma had paid for it or because she didn't want the calories? Probably both.

Rio glared at him, like she'd read his mind. He hadn't said a word!

"How's college, then?" Yuuma asked. "Blast and a half?"

This freed Sakuta from her glare.

"It's all right. Most days nothing really happens."

"I think you're legally required to enjoy it, Azusagawa. Since Sakurajima's there."

"Nah, we have different majors. We really only see each other at lunch."

And since Mai was famous nationwide, she was very busy and often not attending classes at all.

"Hmm, that makes sense. You any better?" Yuuma glanced at Rio.

"I'm…" She thought for a moment. "Doing all right."

She used the same phrase Sakuta had gone with.

"I thought college was all about joining clubs and going wild at mixers!"

That was a pretty biased impression, but some people certainly were doing that. He knew students who were very focused on their social lives. They acted like a person's value was determined by the number of mixers they'd been to and the number of phone numbers they'd amassed.

"Maybe other people, but not me."

Sakuta hadn't joined a club or gone to any of those mixer things.

"No one's even invited me."

"Your fault for dating the cutest girl in the world," Rio said.

This was true. Everyone around knew Sakuta and Mai were a thing, so no one was about to invite them to singles parties.

"But how you faring, Futaba? Been to any?"

At the very least, she'd yet to mention anything like that.

"Of course not," she said with a snort. At the same time, it sounded like she meant that in a self-deprecating way.

"It wouldn't be the end of the world if you did, you know…"

Rio's self-esteem was perpetually a little low. Sakuta had no doubt that if they ran a straw poll of the customers in this restaurant, a solid 80 percent would deem her attractive. Since starting college, she'd begun wearing natural makeup and bringing out her hidden charms. Rio insisted this was just his imagination.

"But you *have* been invited?" Yuuma said, swallowing the last of his whitebait. He hadn't missed that there was more to her denial than first met the eye.

"Well, yes…," she admitted. Reluctantly.

"First I've heard of it," Sakuta said.

"Why would I tell you?"

"We're friends?"

"I had a cram school shift that day."

"And you used that as an excuse to get out of it."

"……"

Sakuta deliberately spelled it out, which earned him another baleful glare. He turned to Yuuma for help but only got the sound of slurped soup. His friend was pretending not to notice his predicament.

Luckily, Sakuta was saved by the buzz of a vibrating phone.

"That yours, Futaba?" Yuuma asked, already checking his own.

Rio dug her phone out of her purse, and sure enough, she was getting a call.

She glanced at the display.

"Classmate."

"Don't mind us," Yuuma said, gesturing for her to answer.

"Sorry," she said, and got up. "What is it?" she asked, walking toward the door.

"Looks like Futaba is a proper college kid after all," Yuuma said, looking pleased. *Anyone* calling Rio was good news.

"Well, she *is* a college student."

"Fair."

Yuuma didn't say it outright, but Sakuta knew what he meant. Rio had spent high school alone in the science lab, so this was an obvious improvement.

"The students at the cram school really trust her, too."

Sakuta often saw her after classes answering questions. On the other hand, both of Sakuta's students tended to bolt the second class ended.

"I heard."

"From her?"

"As if she'd say? She ain't you."

"I wouldn't, either!"

"Basketball Club kid, two years under us, second-year now. He's one of Futaba's students."

So he would've been a first-year when Sakuta and Yuuma were third.

"He's taller than me, so I bet you've seen him around. I bumped into him at the station last week—dude got even taller. Bet he's nearly six foot three."

"Mm, I think there is one such giant."

Sakuta had been on the elevator with him and gone, *Damn.*

"But I'm glad you're both doing well."

"You're the one who did a six-month disappearing act. Training, my ass."

Sakuta and Rio were the ones who were relieved that all was well with their friend.

"Looks like she's enjoying herself," Yuuma said, watching Rio on her call.

Rio had her back to them, but her shoulders were shaking. Whoever she was talking to must have made her laugh. She probably had an awkward grin on her face, too.

"…Did you ever consider going to college?" Sakuta asked.

"I guess a part of me did. Most people I know are going."

Kanagawa Prefecture had a 60 percent higher-education rate. That was the sort of fun fact you naturally acquired working at a cram school.

But from his own experience at Minegahara, far more students were studying for exams, trying to get themselves into college. That 60 percent was just how many succeeded, and it didn't include all the students who ended up having to sit exams again the next year. Sakuta was pretty sure something like 90 percent wanted to go to college. Only a handful were immediately entering the workforce like Yuuma, one or two per class. Anyone not in those groups was likely headed to a vocational school.

"But now that I'm working, it's actually a relief."

Sakuta surmised this was because his friend could finally ease the burden on the single mother who'd raised him. Yuuma had already planned to go down this path when they'd met back in the first year of high school. He'd decided it all on his own. And he'd achieved his goal. That *would* be a relief. No other word could capture it better. And Sakuta was relieved to hear it.

When Sakuta didn't immediately say anything, Yuuma joked, "Plus, no more nodding off in boring classes."

"Firefighters don't study?"

"When we're not out in the field, we're learning about how crews handled tricky problems in the past, et cetera. And there's a ton of drills and training."

"You act like that's fun."

"Muscles never betray you."

Sakuta couldn't relate.

"Well then, keep protecting our town."

"I will."

There was a lull in the conversation, so they took a sip of water to fill it.

"Oh, right. Sakuta."

"Mm?"

"You got anything to say to me?"

"Good work surviving training. Congrats on getting a posting? That cover it?"

"I knew you hadn't noticed."

"What?"

"I ain't telling now. It'll be funnier that way."

"Uhhh…"

He was lost. What was it he'd missed? Some schoolyard prank? Was there a note with an insult on his back?

Yuuma made it sound significant, but before Sakuta could press the point, Rio hung up and came back.

"Sorry," she said again, taking a seat.

"Friend?" Yuuma asked.

"Mm…there are classes where you do experiments and write reports on them, but you've gotta pair up for it. And that meant we got to talking…"

She wasn't doing anything bad, but her story sounded more like an excuse. She always spoke clear and emphatically, but this felt like prying teeth.

"What's she like?"

"She's from Hokkaido. Doesn't really know her way around Tokyo yet. All these trains. Asked me to show her around, but it's not like I know…"

Sakuta had heard this much before.

"I've been telling her to introduce us, but Futaba won't make it happen."

"Why would I let her meet you?"

"Gotta ask her to look after you."

"Yep." Yuuma nodded.

"What are you talking about?" she asked before letting out an exasperated sigh. "I guess I could ask…"

"Oh?" He got his hopes up.

"Would you like to meet two boys who both have girlfriends?"

She was fully back in her stride now.

"You're never letting us meet, huh?"

"You two would definitely put ideas in her head."

Rio got up.

"There's a line outside. We should get going," she said, and she took out her wallet.

Ten minutes later, they were walking along the Katase Eastside Beach. They hadn't made further plans, and none of them had specifically suggested heading to the shore. They'd just eaten their fill, started walking, and wound up here.

During swimming season, beaches in sight of Enoshima would be covered in people and seaside stalls.

But with fall settling in, all that hubbub was forgotten, and people were few and far between. Young couples strolled hand in hand along the surf. Married couples were walking their dogs. College crowds sat on the steps between the sand and the street, talking.

The coast curved gently, like a crescent moon. Today was the spring tide, and the sands went all the way to Enoshima itself.

They walked across lands usually below sea level, toward the island opposite.

A pair of college girls heading the same way were chatting.

"Crazy, we can walk to Enoshima!"

"It's not an island anymore! It's part of the mainland!"

They were competing to see who could upload the best photo. Electronic shutter sounds filled the autumn air.

"Lemme take one," Yuuma said, hoisting his phone. He stuck his arm all the way out so Sakuta and Rio could fit in the shot. He took several pictures. "Let's call it *Arrival at Enoshima*," he said as he showed them the best result.

"We've been there before."

"But always crossing up above."

It was fun seeing the Benten Bridge from below. Sakuta had never realized it walking across, but from down here, it really was a massive structure. Obviously—it was well over four hundred yards long.

"We go too slow and the waters'll roll back in," Rio warned as she began walking back to the beach.

She had a point; it did seem like the water was getting closer.

The tides really were a fascinating phenomenon. The line between the ocean and the land would change by dozens of yards, hundreds.

He and Yuuma followed Rio across the wet sands. They chatted about what they'd been up to, trading stories from high school, laughing and clapping at the dredged-up memories, allowing themselves to wander on meaningless tangents. The smell of the sea washed over them. The three of them basked in the familiar glow, even as Benten Bridge loomed over their return.

They whiled away the time like this, with no real goal in mind. Before they knew it, it was past two.

"You said you had work at three?"

"Yep."

"Mm."

Sakuta's and Rio's answers overlapped. They both had private lessons scheduled at the cram school.

"And you're off duty, Kunimi. You should go home and get some real rest."

With flawless timing, Yuuma yawned.

"I'm definitely not used to these long shifts yet," he admitted. "Always pretty sleepy after one ends."

He yawned again and flashed a sheepish grin.

They headed back to the station they'd met up at and boarded a train. They rode three stops to Fujisawa Station. This was Yuuma's stop, and the cram school where Sakuta and Rio worked was certainly close enough to classify as "by the station." A few minutes' walk at most.

Outside the gates, they said good-bye and waved Yuuma off. They watched him mingle with the crowds; he was soon out of sight.

"Firefighting sounds hard."

"He's built for it."

"You definitely aren't."

With that remark, Rio started walking to the north side of the station, where the cram school was. Sakuta kept pace.

"It's my dream to become Santa Claus," he said.

"See, this is why you started having visions of miniskirt Santas."

"I wish that's all it was."

That would be preferable. Vastly.

But the miniskirt Santa he'd met that Monday had been far too real.

"Only you could see her, right?"

That was true. But the words she'd said stuck in his ears. He remembered the timbre of her voice. Felt her breath on him. She had been there, with him. He was sure of it.

He'd called Rio that day and told her all about it. This was why she'd brought it up just now.

"What do you think that was?" he asked. He'd still only seen her the once.

"If she called herself Touko Kirishima, then she probably is."

Rio clearly just couldn't be bothered.

"Take this seriously, Futaba."

"It's closest to Sakurajima's case."

No one else had been able to perceive her—or even remember she existed.

"But you know that better than I do, Azusagawa."

"True."

"I looked into Touko Kirishima online, but nobody mentioned anything about miniskirt Santas."

The only appearances she ever made were exclusively on video-sharing websites. There were no reports of anyone seeing her in person. Some of her videos did feature a silhouette, but nothing that could positively identify her. And there was no guarantee that silhouette was even hers.

"All my investigation dug up was extremely dubious-sounding speculation."

"Like how she might actually be Mai?"

Takumi Fukuyama—a friend of his at college—had told him that one.

"Or she's an AI."

"People sure do have wild imaginations."

"But if you look at it another way, it's actually pretty weird that there's so little real info in this day and age. Like, even if the papers and TV keep a criminal's name under wraps, you can usually find that somewhere online."

Anyone and everyone could drop word whenever they felt like it— both handy and a headache. Truth and lies could be found everywhere in equal measure.

"But if she's like Mai and no one can actually perceive Touko Kirishima, then it makes sense she'd be able to keep her identity secret."

"In which case, she's been living like a ghost for two whole years. That's how long she's been a thing."

Sakuta had first heard the name Touko Kirishima in high school, straight from Mai's lips. A girl from her agency had recommended a video, and she'd started watching it.

He had never imagined he might one day meet the performer in question, much less when she was dressed as a miniskirt Santa.

The most thought he ever gave it was, *Is that the latest rage?*

"Two years as a ghost would be brutal."

Sakuta had learned firsthand what being imperceptible was like. Everyone walking right past him. No one responding when he spoke. Ignoring his touch.

Only a few hours of this had nearly driven him around the bend. Two whole years of that—just the thought made him shudder.

But there was a big difference from Mai's and Sakuta's cases— Touko Kirishima *did* exist, online. People had not forgotten her and could still perceive her work.

Perhaps that had made all the difference.

"Why is it you want the miniskirt Santa to be real?"

"I'd rather she stay a complete and total stranger."

That was ideal.

No connection to him, no further contact, no disruptions to his life—he'd much rather go on living like nothing was happening.

Unfortunately, he'd already met her—a miniskirt Santa calling herself Touko Kirishima.

And the worst part was what she'd said to him.

Sakuta had met the miniskirt Santa—Touko Kirishima—six days ago.

Monday, October 24.

His college campus.

Before first period even began.

Between the rows of gingko trees, students streamed down the path to class.

He'd just seen Uzuki Hirokawa off after her surprise early graduation.

"Aww, such a shame. And after I let her read the room," a certain girl said, appearing next to him.

She was dressed as a miniskirt Santa. Her long lashes fluttered. She saw him staring and turned to him.

They'd exchanged a few words before she gave her name.

"I'm Touko Kirishima."

All that was just her saying hello. The real meat of the matter came after, sandwiched by the conversation that followed.

"You made it sound like Zukki's Adolescence Syndrome was *your* doing."

He'd gotten the ball rolling, voicing his concern.

"That was the intent!"

She looked baffled that the events could have been interpreted any other way.

"Really?" he asked, just to be sure.

"Really," she said, all smiles.

"How is that possible?"

"You didn't know? Santa Claus brings presents to all the good children."

"Does that mean I've been good, and you came to see me?"

Sadly, it wasn't Christmastime yet. Halloween hadn't even come yet.

"You've got your eyes peeled, trying to figure out who Santa really is—you might just be a bad boy."

Boots clicking, Touko made a circuit around him. She moved at a steady pace, her eyes never leaving him.

The whole while, students were all around them, walking quickly down the path to make sure they got to class in time.

No one noticed the attractive miniskirt Santa. A few of them gave Sakuta puzzled looks, wondering why he was just standing there.

"Do me a favor," he said when the footsteps were right behind him.

"What?"

"Stop handing out presents."

As he spoke, she came into view on his left. She kept moving until she was right in front of him—then she turned to face him.

"Okay," she said.

"That easy?"

He hadn't expected her to agree.

"I mean, I'm already out of presents."

Touko held up her white sack. It was clearly empty. Nothing left inside.

"How many were in that?"

"Five? Ten? Or more than that?"

"This many," she said, holding up an index finger and pointing it at him.

"One?"

"Hardly," she said with a laugh, like he had to be joking.

"Ten?"

"Bzzt, wrong."

He really didn't want to go up another digit, but she didn't leave him much choice.

"A hundred…?"

Not a number he even wanted to imagine.

"Not even close. I'm Santa Claus!"

"A thousand?"

"More like ten million."

"……"

The sheer scale of that number was so vast. At first, he couldn't even grasp it. Not a handful or even a bunch but ten damn million.

"See? Him and her and her and him and him and her," Touko said, pointing at people in the crowd. "I gave them *all* presents."

She looked very pleased with herself.

Did everyone she pointed at have some sort of Adolescence Syndrome, like Uzuki? Was that true for ten million people not here? His mind couldn't even process the thought.

"Santa, you're only supposed to work on Christmas Day," he managed, after a long silence.

"Well, they're the ones who wanted presents. She's one of them."

Touko was looking his way, but not at him. Her gaze went past where he stood to someone behind him.

Who was she talking about?

He slowly turned around.

A college girl was walking at the edge of the path.

He recognized her.

Ikumi Akagi. His classmate back in junior high.

Sakuta had no idea if everything Touko Kirishima had said to him was true.

She'd given out Adolescence Syndrome like it was a present—because that's what Santa Claus did. To ten million people…Ikumi Akagi among them.

A ridiculous story.

A huge pain in the ass.

"What's your take on it, Futaba?"

"We can't prove that it's true or prove that it isn't."

"I guess not."

That's where they were at right now.

"But if it is true, doesn't it back up what you said before?" he asked. "When I talked to you about Zukki, you said the Adolescence Syndrome was affecting all college students, making them all read the room."

When he'd first heard that, it had sounded like far too many people, and he'd almost laughed. Rio herself hadn't really believed that theory. But if ten million people were affected, then "all college students" no longer sounded so absurd.

"If it was real, what would you do?" she asked.

"Be very surprised?"

"Not gonna be a big ole hero and step in to cure 'em all?"

"All ten million?"

"Yes, all ten million."

"Afraid I'll be too busy flirting with Mai."

He'd never been the heroic type, and this world didn't seem like it needed any heroism. Several days had passed since he'd spoken to Touko, and they'd been just like any other. Adolescence Syndrome was hardly causing a worldwide panic.

Nobody was begging for help. Villains were not out and about wrecking everything. Even if superheroes did exist, they would've closed up shop.

"You say that, but you are worried about her, right? Ikumi Akagi, was it?"

"Less worried and more…it's just been bugging me. This whole time."

"……?" Rio looked at him, waiting.

"The day of the entrance ceremony. Why'd she call out to me?"

Was it possible she actually had something to say?

——*"You're Azusagawa, right?"*

——*"Akagi?"*

——*"Yeah. Been a while."*

Had she meant to say more? If Nodoka and Uzuki hadn't caught up with him, would she have?

"And now in hindsight, you're thinking that might have been connected to Adolescence Syndrome?"

Rio could see where he was going with this.

Adolescence Syndrome was all about mysterious phenomena that nobody would ever believe. But in junior high, Sakuta had publicly insisted it was real. Ikumi had been in the room for that.

If she was mixed up in something strange and in trouble, if she'd tried to turn to him for help—that idea wasn't so far-fetched. Who else would believe her? If she was affected, Ikumi knew just how rare that was.

"I'm probably overthinking it."

"Almost definitely," Rio said. "If I was her, you're the last person I'd go to."

"Why?"

"She didn't help you, but now she's got the nerve to ask you for help?"

"Oh. Well, if she can still make those kinds of distinctions, it can't be that bad."

"I think it's more a point of pride."

Sakuta got that. And she knew that he did, but she said it anyway. For emphasis.

"What's she been like since?"

"Akagi?"

"Mm."

"Haven't seen her since I met the miniskirt Santa."

Ikumi was probably attending classes, but she was in the nursing school, so their paths didn't cross often. They barely even saw each other around campus. He'd fully intended to make contact, but the opportunity had yet to arise.

"Maybe it's for the best if you don't run into her again."

"Mm?"

"I'm saying, you're better off having nothing to do with either Touko Kirishima or Ikumi Akagi."

"Well, glad my friends still worry about me."

By this point, they'd reached the building that housed the cram school.

"I just don't want you coming to me for advice," Rio said, punching the elevator button.

Four, three—the flashing numbers of the floor indicators were steadily coming down.

"I know saying this won't change anything…"

"What?"

"If you keep this up, it'll be just like…"

"Like what?"

"Like how detectives constantly stumble across murders."

The bell rang, and the elevator doors opened.

"And what advice do you have for me there?"

"If you run into the miniskirt Santa again, get her phone number."

With that, Rio stepped into the elevator. He followed her.

"I've got a girlfriend. Am I allowed to ask girls for their number?"

"That's what rascals do," Rio said with a smirk as she pushed the button for their floor.

2

Between hanging out with Yuuma, his class at the cram school, *and* a shift at the restaurant, Sunday was a long one. Yet Monday still came at him in the morning.

A depressing way to start the week.

He was woken up by his cat, Nasuno, stepping on his face. He made breakfast for Kaede, got ready to go, and left the house—all part of his typical routine.

But that's where routine ended.

His route to school was not at all typical.

The view out the window wasn't the one he'd been staring at for six months. From the moment he left home, everything he'd seen was new.

For good reason—Sakuta was sitting in the passenger seat of a *car.*

Mai was driving. And obviously, that meant they were taking a different route.

She'd called shortly after his shift last night. "I'm filming at the studio in town tomorrow. I'll be driving in, so I can drop you off at campus."

A morning driving date with Mai. He wasn't about to turn *that* down.

And in a car, they didn't have to worry about prying eyes. Didn't have to worry about anyone eavesdropping on their conversation. This moment was for them and them alone.

"Will you be back late tonight, Mai?"

"Yeah, almost certainly. Why?"

"I don't have a shift, so I thought I'd have dinner waiting for you."

But if she'd be back late, that wouldn't work.

"You have work tomorrow?" she asked. "Which one?"

"Cram school."

"Then you'll be back by nine?"

"If I rush, I can make it by eight thirty."

"Go ahead and walk. I'll cook for you. Any requests?"

Everything Mai cooked was good, so this was a tough choice. As he dithered, a very cross voice answered for him.

"Curry."

Putting on his best scowl, he turned to the back seat. Nodoka was sitting there, glowering even more than he was.

"How long have you been there, Toyohama?"

"The whole time!"

"You shouldn't have said anything."

"I let you have the passenger seat, didn't I? But were you grateful? Nooooope!"

"Thanks for ruining our morning driving date."

"Then curry it is," Mai said.

Nodoka's proposal had somehow won out.

"Do I not get a vote?"

"Serves you right."

He could see Nodoka's triumphant grin in the mirror. Despicable.

"You met up with Futaba yesterday, right?"

"I did. And Kunimi."

"What'd she say?"

Mai left out the specifics, but he knew what she meant. There was no need to make her elaborate. She was asking about the miniskirt Santa—about Touko Kirishima.

The way nobody else could see her was an awful lot like Mai's own case of Adolescence Syndrome. That's probably why it was bugging her.

"Futaba suggested I try to get her phone number."

"You sure do collect female friends."

Mai's words were barbed.

"But you're the only one I *love*."

"I'll allow it. I suppose asking this Touko Kirishima directly is the quickest solution."

"Is this the miniskirt Santa you met?" Nodoka interjected. She didn't look up from her phone and didn't seem that interested. "You sure you weren't just daydreaming? Nobody would wander around campus dressed like that. Even if they were invisible."

A sensible statement, really.

"She's calling you out, Mai."

To be fair, Mai hadn't gone for the miniskirt Santa look. Her outfit had been even sexier—a proper bunny-girl outfit. And she'd worn it to the library instead of a college campus.

The moment they hit a red light, Mai reached out to pinch his cheek.

"Owww! That hurts, Mai!"

Mai was smiling pleasantly, but the look in her eyes warned him not to blab.

"True, it is supposed to be our little secret... Ow! Mai, the light! It's green!"

The car in front pulled out, so Mai let go of him. She stepped on the gas and eased forward.

"Oh, Toyohama," Sakuta said, rubbing his cheek.

"What?"

"Did Hirokawa ever meet Touko Kirishima?"

Uzuki's popularity wave had been kicked off by a commercial for wireless earphones that used a Touko Kirishima song. Uzuki had done an a cappella cover of it that got everyone talking.

And if she'd been given Adolescence Syndrome as a present, they might have met.

"She said she wanted to say hi but never got the chance."

"Huh."

"The label that approved the song licensing said they do everything through e-mail."

That was the end of that. No way in or out. Any questions he had would have to wait until he ran into her again. *If* that happened at all.

"Guess you'll have to talk to that girl from your junior high."

"Yeah."

He wasn't thrilled about the prospect, but it was a more tangible lead than chasing a miniskirt Santa who might not even exist. Ikumi Akagi was definitely a student at his college.

The view out the windows was starting to look familiar. Up ahead, he could see Kanazawa-hakkei Station, the nearest stop.

They'd left Fujisawa only forty minutes ago. This moment with Mai was all too fleeting.

"Don't fall asleep in class," she said as she let them off in front of the station.

"If I get to dream about you, I'd rather sleep," he joked just before shutting the door.

He watched her mouth an insult, then drive off with a smile.

3

After second period, Sakuta stopped by the ATM, then stepped into the cafeteria to find it absolutely packed with hungry students.

He did not see an empty seat anywhere.

Undiscouraged, he kept looking.

Then his eyes found a back he recognized. That half-up hair bun was definitely Miori Mitou, a relatively new acquaintance.

She was alone at a table for four. He approached and asked, "Mind if I join you?"

Miori looked up, udon hanging from her lips. She slurped up the noodles, then chewed. Only when she swallowed did she make a show of annoyance and say, "I'd rather you didn't."

The gleam in her eyes made it clear this was payback for their first conversation.

"I shall anyway," he said, his tone as contrived as hers. He sat down across the table from her.

"You alone today, Azusagawa?"

"Look again. I'm with *you*."

"Oh, you *are* obnoxious."

He opened up his bento box and started eating. He'd only bothered bringing it to the lunchroom because they had hot tea for free. And if there was someone to eat with, all the better.

"You alone today, Mitou?"

Usually when he saw her here, she was with other girls from her major.

"Look again," she said. "I'm with *you*."

"Oh, you *are* obnoxious."

It seemed polite to respond in kind.

"Mai's working?"

"Today, yesterday, and the day before."

Yet she was still earning enough credits. Mad respect.

"Aww. Fine, take Mai's, too."

Miori dramatically produced two large jars out of her bag. They were both about the right size to carry one-handed. One was labeled STRAWBERRY JAM, and the other BLUEBERRY.

Why the jam surprise?

"Is it Jam Day?"

Maybe there was some sort of jam gift custom, like how people handed out chocolate on Valentine's.

"Jam Day is April twentieth, I think."

"It exists?!"

He would have to look up how *that* happened. If he remembered to.

"I brought these back for you. Manami got her license, and to celebrate, we all went on a drive."

"This the girl who didn't invite you to the beach?"

"Okay, that's *extra* obnoxious."

She pointed her chopsticks at him sternly.

"Bad manners," he said.

"Where do you think we went?" she asked, putting her chopsticks down.

"Good question," he said while reaching for the jars. The answer was written right there on the back, next to the nutritional label. "Nagano?"

The manufacturer was based out of Karuizawa.

"More specifically, the Azusagawa Rest Area."

She fixed him with an extremely broad grin.

"Not that funny," he said, putting the jam down.

Certainly not a joke worth being smug about.

"I'll be taking this back." Miori snatched the blueberry jam away.

He didn't want her confiscating the strawberry, too, so he put it away in his rucksack. It was highly probable he'd put his foot in his mouth again.

"Thanks for the jam. Your friend—Miyuki, was it?"

"Manami."

"You've patched things over with her?"

When he'd first met Miori, she'd been in a bind—the guy Manami was after had been far more interested in *her*. Or more accurately, Sakuta had thrown that idea out there, and Miori had more or less admitted it.

"We're all in college now. That much, we can manage. No one benefits from a long-running beef."

Miori rolled her eyes and then noisily slurped up the last of her udon.

"She invited me to a mixer today. Hot guys from a top city school are gonna be there, apparently."

Chewing her udon, she managed an awkward smile.

"I may have mentioned it? She promised to set up a mixer to make up for the beach incident."

"I vaguely remember."

"I assumed it was an empty promise." Miori winced. "And since it's *for* me, I can't bow out," she muttered, looking like a kid who'd been served food they hate. She didn't want to eat it but knew her parents wouldn't let her leave the table until she did. No escape!

"Well, you're in college now. You'll have to manage. No one benefits from a long-running beef."

"Oh, you *are* annoying."

After her words were turned against her, Miori leaned back in her chair, disgruntled. She pursed her lips and glared up at him through her lashes.

When he just kept on eating, she grumbled "Annoying" again.

This was weirdly charming, and he couldn't help but approve. She wasn't *trying* to be cute, but that's just how her every gesture and mannerism came off.

The way she followed the latest makeup trends and dressed nice but not flashy—he was pretty sure Miori did that all for *herself.* Because she liked it. She wanted to. That's why it didn't feel phony. And the men around her were drawn to that—which was why they kept glancing her way.

Since he'd first met her, she'd acted the same way with everyone—while other girls were more initially guarded. And men misread that more often than not, assuming they had a shot with her.

And once they started nursing that faint hope, they stopped paying attention to any other signals. So many never realized that they'd never grown any closer than they'd started out.

Sakuta was a "potential friend," and that suited him just fine. He enjoyed bumping into her on campus and chatting now and again. Having friends like that wasn't bad at all.

But his chain of thought was interrupted by a friendly voice.

"Oh, there you are, Azusagawa!"

Takumi Fukuyama had appeared bearing the cafeteria's signature rice bowl. He was in the same major as Sakuta, which was how they'd gotten to know each other.

"A-and Mitou?!" Takumi yelped. He'd only just gotten a clear view of her.

"Um…," she said as he took a seat next to Sakuta.

"Takumi Fukuyama! First-year statistical science major, same as Azusagawa here."

"Miori Mitou, first-year international management. But we're in the same core classes, right? You were at that party."

By this she meant the gathering at the start of the term—where she and Sakuta had met.

"That I was!" Takumi leaned forward, far too excited that she'd remembered him.

"I'll leave you kids to get acquainted," Sakuta said, packing up his empty lunch box and rising to leave. Miori was being cross with him, so a hasty retreat seemed in order.

But Takumi's hand clamped down on his shoulder.

"Stay put, Azusagawa. I need a favor and was looking for you."

"With a *yokoichi-don*?"

This was the school special, and he'd ordered one with extra rice.

"Can't fight on an empty stomach."

"Finding me isn't war, so you could have managed."

Sakuta had missed his chance to leave, so Miori stood up instead.

"I'll leave you kids to get acquainted," she said with a smirk, and she took her tray off to the dish return.

"You sure, Fukuyama?"

"About what?"

"Your shot at getting to know Mitou."

"You think I'm ready for that?"

"You want a girlfriend so bad I figured you were always ready."

"If I was ready, I'd have a girlfriend by now."

"Fair."

"You free today?"

"I got classes till fourth period."

"I know. I mean after."

"I'll be busy washing my cat."

"Then come to this mixer instead. We got a man out sick and gotta make up the numbers."

"Did you not hear me?"

If Nasuno didn't get that bath soon, she'd start to smell like a zoo.

"You remember Ryouhei Kodani? The international management dude a year above us, who showed up at the core curriculum class party even though he's not in that class?"

"No memory of him whatsoever."

Miori was the only new name he'd acquired in the bar near Yokohama Station. Arguably, he'd also picked up the name of Miori's friend Manami. Then again, he'd been pretty sure her name was Miyuki until, like, a minute ago.

"Anyway, I'm in Chinese with Kodani. We were talking about mixers, and he went and set one up."

"Sounds too good to be true. Watch yourself."

"And all three girls are from the nursing school," Takumi said, as if this was of grave import.

"Are they…?"

That *did* get his attention. Very good timing.

"We're talking nurses, man, nurses! You should be way more excited."

"About future nurses? They're just college girls right now."

They were no different from anyone else at this point in time.

"What, do nurses not do it for you?"

He looked at Sakuta as if it had never once occurred to him that this was even possible.

"If you'd said miniskirt Santas, I'd have been there in a flash."

"That'd work, yep."

Takumi nodded emphatically.

But it wasn't like Sakuta had zero interest in nurses. Especially given his interest in a certain someone. Ikumi Akagi was in the nursing program here.

Odds that she would be at this mixer were slim at best, but people in the same major as her might know what she was up to. If he could get them talking, it might be worth it.

But since Sakuta was dating Mai, going to mixers at all was questionable. Whatever the motives, he did not belong there.

He weighed his options.

"You gotta come, Azusagawa!"

"Won't bringing a taken man spoil things?"

The goal wasn't exactly to make friends. Sometimes it might turn out that way, but mixers were primarily events for singles looking to hook up.

"The way I see it, that's one less rival."

"Meanwhile, I just sit there basting in the girls' scorn? No thanks."

From their perspective, it was the same as having one less guy. And he did not want to subject himself to that.

"You don't care if I never get a nurse girlfriend?"

"Not really, no."

"I'm begging you!"

Takumi slapped his palms together.

"Mai would never approve."

"But what if she does?"

Takumi was not about to let this drop. Surely, there were other people he could ask. But arguing that wouldn't get him anywhere.

"Fine, I'll give her a call and see. If she says no, you'll just have to deal."

"Cool."

Now he just had to ask Mai and get himself chewed out.

He assumed that would happen—but it didn't.

Mai's answer was nothing like what he'd assumed.

4

Long story short, Mai's approval was granted with shocking ease.

Before afternoon classes began, he'd swung by the pay phones near the campus clock tower and called her number. He figured she'd be at a shoot and unable to answer. But she picked up on the first ring.

"What?"

Mai had been checking a text from her manager between shots.

She seemed surprised to hear from him, so he patiently walked her through it.

"Got invited to a mixer."

"And?"

"Someone dropped out last minute, so it's today."

"So?"

"The girls are from the nursing school here. I still shouldn't go, right?"

He really sweated that last line.

"Why not?" Mai said, like this was no skin off her back.

"I mean, I can't," he said, vetoing his own proposal.

"Sakuta, if you blow this chance, you'll never get another."

"You should still stop me. You're my girlfriend!"

"I'm granting you special permission, just this once."

"Still...," he fretted.

"You're the one who asked me," she scoffed. "Why are you trying to back out of it?"

They had definitely swapped positions somewhere along the line.

"You're sure?"

"If you're this reluctant, I'll allow it."

She sounded pleased.

"What if I was super eager?"

"I'd insist you come see me right now."

She let out a mischievous laugh.

"I might've preferred that."

"We're filming. You'd be in the way. Stay put."

"Aww."

"I hope you figure something out," she added, the emotion draining from her voice.

He knew right away she was talking about Ikumi Akagi. The moment Sakuta mentioned the nursing school, she'd understood why he'd brought this mixer up. And while fully aware of that, she had toyed with him for a while first.

"Not getting my hopes up," he said. "But I'll give it a shot."

Even if these girls were from her major, they might not know anything about Ikumi. There were tons of students in every major, and you never matched names to faces for the majority. Even if one of Ikumi's friends happened to be at the mixer, it wasn't exactly the sort of scene where you could sit and talk for any length of time about someone who wasn't even there.

Best he could hope for was to say, "Oh yeah, there's a girl called Ikumi Akagi in the nursing school, right? I went to junior high with her," and sound like he was bragging about being from here.

"Saying that you're going in with low expectations is just mean to the girls who'll be there."

"Then I guess I'll carry a faint hope."

"Maybe they'll be cute!" Mai said, playing along.

"Fukuyama says they're all cute."

"Cuter than me?"

"I couldn't handle that."

"Argh, wardrobe call. Gotta go."

She instantly snapped back to work mode, and he heard a woman talking behind her. Her stylist and makeup artist must have stepped into her trailer.

"Knock 'em dead."

"Will do. Bye."

And she hung up.

And thus, Sakuta was allowed to participate in the mixer with nary a word of scolding.

When fourth-period core mathematics ended, he and Takumi got up and left together. Down the teeming corridors, down the stairs, and out the building they went.

The gingko lane was packed with students heading home. The procession continued on the far side of the gates, along the tracks to Kanazawa-hakkei Station.

On the sunset-drenched platform, an express bound for Haneda Airport had just pulled in, and they managed to squeeze through the doors in time.

They stood at the door, gazing through the window.

"I'm starting to tense up," Takumi said. He was being completely serious. They'd just reached Kanazawa-bunko Station. Only one more stop.

"I know a good way to relax."

"Yeah? What?" Takumi took the bait.

"First, put your index fingers in the corners of your mouth."

"Like this?"

"Then turn them out, pulling your lips to both sides."

"Anh?"

Takumi did exactly what he was told.

"Now say 'Kanazawa-bunko.'"

"Kanazawa-unko."

"Ha! Made you say *poop*."

With his lips pried open, he couldn't make a *b* sound.

The doors closed, and they pulled out of the station.

"......"

Takumi took his fingers out of his mouth, quietly waiting for a justification.

"Weird, that got a big laugh at my elementary school."

"We're in college?"

"Feel free to bust that out at the mixer if you can't think of anything to say."

"I'll do absolutely everything in my power to avoid that."

They rode the rest of the way to Yokohama Station in silence.

*   *   *

They made their way through the hub's crowds to the JR Negishi Line. They took that train one more stop to Sakuragicho Station.

Past the gates, they used the east exit and immediately spotted the lights of the Landmark Tower and the coastal shopping district. And of course, the colorful illumination of the Ferris wheel. One of Yokohama's signature views. This much was just typical Sakuragicho Station.

But today was October 31.

The costumed crowds in the square outside had transformed the place into an enchanting wonderland. The pumpkin festival's popularity had reached the youth of this town, too.

Halloween had not been on Sakuta's mind at all, so he was taken aback.

Wizards, vampires, Red Riding Hoods, and popular movie and manga characters surrounded them. There were even a few people wearing famous politician masks, likely as a joke.

Several groups had phones out and were taking pictures; some were filming videos. Others were getting into the partying mood and chatting up the opposite sex.

"Stay close to me, Azusagawa."

"If I get separated, I'll just go home."

He had no clue where they were going and no way to get in touch, so it wasn't like he had much choice.

"That's why I'm warning you."

"Should we hold hands?"

"Oh, please."

Takumi stuck out his tongue and headed away from the clearing. Sakuta followed. Despite the size of the crowd, it didn't feel packed— probably because most people weren't moving.

They made steady progress.

But no sooner had he started to relax than he almost bumped into a girl wearing a nurse costume.

They saw each other just in time and stopped inches away.

She was wearing not the plain white angelic outfit common in most hospitals, but an old-fashioned look like the mascot on the lip balm packaging. In true Halloween spirit, she had blood applied to her nose and just below the eyes.

When their eyes met, she looked surprised.

Sakuta wasn't sure why. She was the one in an unusual costume, and he sure hadn't expected to run into her out here.

But when she bobbed her head and turned to leave, her name crossed his lips.

"Akagi...?"

The nurse's back went still.

Quietly, she turned halfway toward him.

Her gaze wavered awkwardly.

Still rattled by running into him here? He was, too. He hadn't prepared for this and didn't know what to say.

And as he struggled to react, Ikumi said, "Sorry, gotta go," and moved away.

He considered stopping her but couldn't think of an excuse.

And she seemed to be moving with purpose. Her path took her right toward the streetlight in the center of the clearing.

Was she meeting someone there?

He thought so at first. But the way she acted suggested otherwise. Ikumi had reached the light and was staring up at the glass pumpkins they'd installed for Halloween. Occasionally, she checked her phone. Was it to keep an eye on the time?

And she was watching the crowd intently, like she was searching for someone. She seemed to be taking this very seriously.

She stuck out like a sore thumb standing there surrounded by partygoers. She was the only person not having fun.

And past her, Sakuta spotted a tiny figure running up to the

pumpkin lantern. It was a little girl dressed as Red Riding Hood, her parents right behind.

"Take a picture with the pumpkin!" she cried, pointing up at the lantern.

As the girl tried to take a step closer—

"Not there!" Ikumi yelped, grabbing her shoulders.

Surprised, the girl stopped.

Then—

—the pumpkin lantern *fell*.

It hit the ground and shattered, sending shards of glass flying in every direction.

The little girl had been less than a yard away.

If Ikumi hadn't stopped her, it would have landed right on her red riding hood. That might not have been fatal, but she definitely would've been hurt.

The wizards and vampires near them stopped chatting and filming and stared at the lantern, the girl, and Ikumi. "Huh?" "What happened?"

Ikumi bent down and asked, "Are you okay?"

"Mm."

Her parents came rushing over. "Miyu, does anything hurt?"

"Nope!"

"Thank you," the father said, bowing to Ikumi, who shook her head.

"Come on, Miyu, thank the nice lady."

"Thank you, lady!"

"You're welcome." She stayed at eye level to give the girl a big smile.

A man patrolling the square came over and started checking if anyone was hurt. He had a Yokohama armband, so he must have been employed by the city.

Once he was sure there were no injuries, he politely asked the crowd to stand back and began cleaning up the shattered glass.

Other staff members brought in some orange cones. They soon had a barrier set up around the lantern. Leaving the first man to handle cleanup, they focused on crowd control.

And the onlookers soon turned back to their own fun.

It was just a fallen lantern.

No one was hurt.

So what did it matter?

Most of them would not even remember it tomorrow.

That was the general feeling.

Sakuta was the only one certain something was very wrong.

This had been downright disturbing. Unnatural.

How had Ikumi known to stop the little girl before the lantern fell?

Like she'd *known* it was going to happen.

"……"

He stared at her from a distance, and when Ikumi noticed, she turned toward him.

Their eyes met again.

But only for an instant.

She quickly broke eye contact and vanished into the sea of Halloween costumes. He lost her behind someone who'd really gone all out on the zombie makeup, and he was unable to find her again.

"What *is* she doing…?" he muttered.

That was all Sakuta had really gotten out of this. What was she doing? What had she done? His head was full of questions.

"I could say the same thing!"

A hand clamped down on his shoulder, and he turned to find Takumi looking out of breath.

"I seriously thought I'd lost you," Takumi said, forcibly turning Sakuta around. "This way, straight ahead."

He got a good grip on Sakuta's rucksack strap and pulled him away to their mixer with the future nurses.

5

Takumi dragged him to a building a good five minutes away from the bustle of the main square.

"This is it," he said after carefully comparing the sign outside with the directions on his phone.

Takumi pulled Sakuta into the elevators. The crowds had thinned out enough that there was no risk of getting lost anymore, but Takumi showed no signs of releasing the rucksack strap.

They rode the elevator to the fourth floor, where the restaurant was waiting. Takumi stopped in front of the floor map, his eyes searching for a creative Japanese cuisine *izakaya*.

Takumi finally released his strap once they were outside the restaurant doors. They pushed through the (extremely modern-looking) hanging curtains.

"Welcome," a young male staff member said with impeccable manners.

"Oh, they're with us," said a bespectacled college guy behind them.

"Kodani!" Takumi raised a hand. "Sorry, we're a bit late."

This must be Ryouhei Kodani.

"This way," Ryouhei said, waving them farther in.

The interior had that upscale, successful shop atmosphere and just the right amount of customers.

"Here we are!" Ryouhei said, at the very back. The meeting place was a semiprivate room with tatami floors, and pits beneath low tables. There were partitions so you couldn't see the next table over. It had enough space for six adults to kick back and relax.

The window offered a view of the night scenery outside. Sadly, it didn't include the Ferris wheel, but the reflections of the city lights on the water were plenty colorful. The view was spectacular.

"C'mon in, sit! The girls said they just reached the station."

Sakuta moved to the back corner, Takumi next to him, and Ryouhei by the door, all on the same side of the table.

"One girl's running late, so we're gonna start when the other two get here," Ryouhei relayed, eyes on his phone. He seemed like he knew what he was doing; he must have set up plenty of mixers before.

When his eyes met Sakuta's, Ryouhei sat up straight on his knees as he formally introduced himself.

"I believe we met before at the core curriculum party, but I'm Ryouhei Kodani. I'm a second-year in international management."

He then held out a small piece of paper—his business card. It said:

Ryouhei Kodani, Social Ecology Club, Ecologist/Director

"Hi, first-year statistical science, Sakuta Azusagawa. I don't have a card."

"That's fine! No formalities needed here."

"I concur."

"A very formal word!"

Ryouhei was the only one laughing.

"So what exactly is a social ecology club?"

He knew what each of those words meant on their own but had never seen them all together like that.

"Oho, are you interested by any chance?" Ryouhei asked like he had been waiting for this exact moment. He pushed up his glasses as he launched into a detailed explanation.

"We're partnered up with similar groups at schools around the city, but basically, the idea is that environmental issues are connected to the systems of control within our society, and we meet up regularly to debate and exchange views related to that concept. Our membership includes a famous sociologist who's been on TV, and our meeting the other day covered the economy, power structures, hierarchies, and the potential that resides in sustainable decision-making, which included discussions about SDGs and ESG investment. We went all night long!"

An absolute stream of unfamiliar jargon poured out of his mouth and left Sakuta even more clueless as to what this club actually did.

"I see," he said, nodding.

"If you want to know more, hit me up any time. Use the code!"

Ryouhei tapped a QR code on his business card.

"But I am relieved you came," he said, sitting back down. "I've been looking for a chance to talk to you."

"Already spoken for."

"Not like that!" Ryouhei laughed heartily. Then—

"Oh, here! Sorry, we're one minute late!"

"That's basically on time."

Two girls came in. One was short with long hair, and the other average height with a bob cut.

"Coming in!"

The smaller one pulled her boots off and stepped into the room first. She wore a dress with a cardigan over it. The other wore a long skirt and a sweater and had a denim jacket slung over her shoulders.

They sat down, and once their drinks arrived, Sakuta's first ever mixer that wasn't for school got underway.

"Thanks for coming out today! It's a pleasure," Ryouhei said.

They all tapped glasses, and he introduced himself. Name, major, year, what he was into these days. Takumi followed suit, and Sakuta after him.

There was a round of applause after each little speech, which helped keep the party going. Ryouhei, Takumi, and the girls were all smiling happily.

Sakuta was doing his part to keep the party going, but half the things they said went in one ear and out the other. Half his mind was on something else.

Specifically, what he'd seen outside the station.

What did Ikumi Akagi's behavior mean?

He couldn't stop thinking about it.

So despite them all introducing themselves, he was none too confident on the girls' names. They were calling each other Chiharu and Asuka, so he went with that.

The smaller one was Chiharu, and the one with an average build was Asuka.

The conversation drifted from introductions to their backgrounds. How close their high schools had been, where they'd gone for sporting matches, speculating if they'd ever run into each other, et cetera.

It was a city college, so lots of students were from Yokohama, or at least Kanagawa Prefecture. Everyone but Takumi here.

There were many moments of finding common ground, a whole chorus of "I know!" and "I've been there!" Chiharu and Asuka were pulling up pics from high school so Takumi could follow along. The first half hour flew by.

Everyone ordered a second drink, and Chiharu was hunting for another photo to share when her phone vibrated.

"Oh, the last girl just reached the station."

If she was on the platform at Sakuragicho Station, it'd take her ten minutes to reach them. The Halloween crowds would slow her down a bit.

"Oh, right, look here!"

Chiharu fired off an answer, then turned her phone to the boys.

The screen was showing a tweet.

Going to a mixer in Sakuragicho on October 31! Might meet the boy of my dreams! #dreaming

"This hashtag dreaming tweet came true!"

Sakuta hadn't heard that phrase often, but he figured it meant the blue word at the end with the symbol in front.

"You go to mixers every day," Asuka said, eating her *yakitori*. "It was bound to come true eventually."

"But I wrote this a month ago! I'd totally forgotten!"

"Are you *sure*?" Ryouhei asked, looking suspicious.

"I swear!" Chiharu cried, a reaction Ryouhei had clearly been hoping for. She insisted he check the tweet's date.

Takumi was laughing at this.

Only Sakuta was totally lost.

"What's this hashtag dreaming thing?" he asked, figuring he'd be left behind otherwise. Chiharu, Asuka, and Ryouhei all looked shocked.

"You've never heard of it?!"

"Azusagawa doesn't have a phone, so he's clueless about these things," Takumi explained.

"For real?"

"Are you insane?"

Chiharu and Asuka looked even more shocked. Like they were encountering an alien life-form.

Sakuta was both real and sane.

"I've had this conversation before, so let's skip to the part where it's over."

"Well, it's new to us!" Chiharu laughed, enjoying his dry humor. She talked all sugary sweet but caught on quick. It was surprisingly fun to talk to her.

"So what is this hashtag thing?" he asked.

Ryouhei stepped in to answer. "It was originally just a tag for dreams you had."

"And tags are markers for particular conversation topics," Takumi added, tipping back his glass.

Ryouhei nodded. "But lately there's a rumor going around that tagged dreams are coming true," he said. "I've looked into it a bit, and there are people out there who dreamed about the next big celebrity scandal or major flooding. Prophetic dreams."

"And I dreamed about this mixer!" Chiharu said, showing him her phone again as if demanding he add her to the list of dreamers.

"Dreams that tell the future, hmm?" Sakuta said, taking a sip of his oolong tea. He wasn't sure if he believed this, but it wasn't entirely out of the question. He knew a high school girl who could run a simulation of several months in the future while she slept. This would be easy enough for the petite devil.

"Nobody's buying it, Chiharu."

"Mean!"

Anyone could see that Chiharu wasn't the least bit upset. It didn't seem like she actually believed the rumors, either. It was just another topic to keep the conversation hopping, no more, no less. For all his claims of looking into it, Ryouhei didn't seem to feel any different. Takumi and Asuka, too—it was just another urban legend. Just a fun thing to chat about. No one would take something that silly seriously.

Any other day, Sakuta would have let it pass himself.

He would have loved to do that today.

The reason he couldn't was simple—he'd seen what Ikumi Akagi did outside the station.

And once the idea was lodged in his head, he couldn't let it drop.

"Um, were there any posts about the square outside Sakuragicho today?"

"Ho-ho. You're more curious about social media than I thought, Azusagawa. Lemme check."

They didn't suspect a thing. To them, it was just part of the fun. A few seconds later, all four found the post.

"'I dreamed a pumpkin lantern fell and hurt a kid dressed as Little Red Riding Hood. Worst dream ever,'" Takumi read.

Sakuta leaned over and checked the day. September 30. One month ago.

He would rather not have known.

How had Ikumi known to stop the girl before the lantern fell?

The mystery was solved.

Just rumors and urban legends. But Ikumi had believed them and saved Little Red Riding Hood.

Like a real hero.

Now he knew how she'd done it, but that still left a lot of mysteries.

If anything, it raised more questions than it answered.

Why had she acted on it?

Had she found the post by accident and just been curious?

Miniskirt Santa had said she'd given Ikumi a present. Was that related?

Before Sakuta could collect his thoughts, Chiharu handed him a menu. "What're you drinking next?" she asked.

He still had half his tea, but he'd probably finish that before the next round arrived, so he ordered a third.

Then he handed the menu back.

She took it from him, making eye contact, cheeks a bit flushed. Eyes filled with curiosity. He could tell where this was going.

"Want some edamame?" he asked, attempting to deflect it.

"Thanks," she said. Chiharu opened the pod and ate the contents with almost palpable relish. "Yum—wait, I was just about to ask you something!"

She dropped the pod, catching on to his ploy. No worming out of it now.

"Azusagawa, is it true you're dating Mai Sakurajima?"

Asuka and Ryouhei were staring at him, too.

Only Takumi was still oohing over how good the tomatoes were.

"Not at all," he fibbed. He was pretty sure this room would get the joke.

"I knew it!" Chiharu played along without missing a beat.

"You are, though!" Takumi yelped, thumping him.

"I guess," he admitted reluctantly. He didn't want to say too much—Mai did *not* need another media frenzy.

"How do you even meet famous people?" Asuka asked.

"Go to the same high school?"

"That wouldn't get you anywhere! There had to be an event that started everything."

Chiharu held out a fake microphone in his direction. She even did the reporter voice.

"I slipped out of class in the middle of exams."

"You did?!" both girls squealed.

"Went out to the empty field."

"And?!" Ryouhei joined them.

"Then I yelled 'I love you!' so loud the whole school heard."

"Seriously?" Chiharu asked in pure disbelief. Asuka and Ryouhei matched her.

"All true. I was in class, watching," a woman's voice said. Not Chiharu or Asuka. And obviously not Sakuta.

He'd heard that voice before…

…but couldn't quite put a face to it.

Sakuta looked up and saw a college girl peering into the room.

"Huh?"

He made a very stupid-sounding noise. Not further words followed it. Just a strangled little croak.

Ignoring him, the third girl took off her shoes and stepped up onto the tatami.

"Sorry I'm late. First-year in nursing school, Saki Kamisato," she said.

Sakuta's brain flashed back to Yuuma's remarks the day before.

——*"You got anything to say to me?"*

——*"I knew you hadn't noticed."*

——*"I ain't telling now. It'll be funnier that way."*

And Sakuta realized that had all been leading up to *this*.

Chapter
2

DISSONANT NOTES

1

The third-period computer literacy class had ended, yet Sakuta lingered in the computer lab. He glumly tapped away at the keyboard, entering numbers in a spreadsheet. The assignment from class was almost over.

"That mixer yesterday was a blast!" Takumi whispered from one seat over. He was mostly talking to himself, spinning his computer stool while fiddling with his phone.

Everyone else had left as soon as the bell rang, so it was just the two of them.

"For everyone but me and Kamisato," Sakuta grumbled, never taking his eyes off the screen.

The mess at yesterday's mixer had been entirely unexpected. A genuine shocker.

Saki Kamisato had gone to the same school as him—Minegahara High. And dated his friend Yuuma. He'd had no idea she was even a student at his college, let alone attending mixers.

Yuuma hadn't mentioned it, and he'd gone six whole months without spotting her.

And she was in the nursing school.

In his mind, she was the polar opposite of a healing influence, so her choice for major was downright mind-boggling.

Sakuta and Saki's unexpected reunion had been a source of infinite amusement to everyone else there, making the party even livelier. The topic naturally turned to high school days, and Sakuta got peppered by questions until the end of the mixer.

Their high school had been located near Kamakura and Enoshima, with a stunning view of the ocean, and was accessible via the famous Enoden train. Add in the fact that Mai Sakurajima also went there and the topic never ran dry.

"An Enoden commute would be rad! Every day could feel like a coming-of-age film."

"I lived close enough that I totally could have gone. I would've sat the exams if I'd known!"

"Seriously."

Chiharu and Asuka had both lived in the area and were extra curious.

"So why didn't you tell us, Saki?" Chiharu asked, shaking her shoulders.

Apparently, Saki had gone all this time without breathing a word about her high school. He could imagine why. Anyone who mentioned Minegahara would get asked about Mai Sakurajima. It wasn't out of the question that people would beg for an introduction. Nobody wanted to deal with that.

"We never did get to the bottom of it! What have you and Kamisato got against each other?" Takumi asked, not once looking up from his phone.

"We're on pretty good terms these days."

They'd been at the same table for an hour and a half. In high school, that would have been unthinkable.

"You call that good?"

"Yep."

She hadn't put it in words or anything, but everyone could tell she didn't like him much. Yet that hadn't managed to spoil the mood.

Like Miori had said, both Sakuta and Saki were just better at these things now. They were in college, after all.

Everyone else had taken the hint and let sleeping dogs lie.

"And what do you actually think of her?" Takumi asked him in the computer lab.

"I'm aware she's got it in for me."

He shrugged before saving his work and attaching it to an e-mail addressed to the professor teaching the computer literacy class.

With that out of the way, Sakuta searched the "dreaming" hashtag. Here he was at a computer, so he might as well put it to use.

"And what's the firefighter boyfriend stuck between you think?"

"I think he'd prefer it if we got along."

No way Yuuma enjoyed hearing them snark about each other. Sakuta didn't think he'd grumbled about her all *that* much, but he'd definitely said a few things.

And Saki had probably complained about him a *lot*. In high school, she'd hated him enough to explicitly order him to stay away from Yuuma.

"Okay, cool."

Takumi seemed to have made up his mind.

"What is?" Sakuta asked, not really caring.

His attention was fully on the computer screen as he skimmed the list of tweets tagged #dreaming. He was definitely not about to read all of these. He limited the search to posts in the last twenty-four hours, and that dropped it down to three hundred—which was still a lot.

Unable to muster the enthusiasm to read through them, he realized Takumi hadn't responded, and he turned to look.

"Fukuyama?"

He was still on his phone.

"You'll find out soon."

Takumi finally glanced up, but only to let out a sinister chuckle.

And before Sakuta could press the point, footsteps came through the door behind him.

It was the clicking of heels.

He swiveled around to look and found the girl they'd been talking about—Saki Kamisato.

She spotted Sakuta and came right toward him. On the way, she said, "Thanks, Fukuyama."

"No problemo."

Takumi spun his chair one last time, then got up, shoving his phone in his pocket. Like he was hiding the evidence that he'd leaked Sakuta's location.

"I'm outta here!" he said, waving his hand. And with that, the snitch left the room.

Leaving Sakuta and Saki alone together.

"……"

"……"

An uncomfortable silence.

But not a long one. Saki spoke first.

"Don't put ideas in Yuuma's head," she said.

"That's a no can do."

"Hah?"

"I left him a voice mail yesterday. Said you showed up late and introduced yourself as the girl with a hunky firefighting boyfriend, totally wrecking the mood of my first real mixer."

And she'd refused to exchange contact info with Takumi and Ryouhei on the grounds that she was already taken. There had definitely been an awkward moment or two.

That was probably why she'd gone through Chiharu or Asuka to get Sakuta's location out of Takumi.

"……"

She was giving him a cross look but didn't lash out.

"They roped me into it to make up the numbers."

"Tell that to Kunimi."

"I will! I'm seeing him later."

"Is that all?"

He couldn't imagine what else she'd want with him, so her answer caught him off guard.

"From me."

"From you?"

She made it sound like someone else wanted to talk to him. An interpretation that proved correct.

Saki ignored his question and headed to the door, saying, "I'm done. Go ahead."

And she was replaced with the last person he expected to see: Ikumi Akagi.

"Thanks, Saki."

"See you tomorrow, Ikumi."

With that, Saki went home.

Ikumi waved her out and watched her go. Only when the footsteps faded did she turn to face Sakuta.

She worked her way through the tables toward him, but not all the way. She stopped a good three seats out.

"Azusagawa. You went to high school with Saki?"

"Akagi. You're friends with Kamisato?"

He noticed they were on a first-name basis. It didn't feel like they were strangers at all.

"Mm. Saki was the first person I talked to here. She helps out occasionally with the volunteer group I founded."

"Educational support?"

"You've heard of it?"

"I saw you recruiting a few times."

"Oh."

Their conversation didn't have much substance. They were just carefully feeling out the distance between them. The mood was kind of tense and both of them were obviously choosing their words with care.

They'd been in the same class in junior high but barely spoken. Neither of them knew exactly how they were meant to interact.

"Didn't think Kamisato was the volunteering type."

"Oh? I think it's very her."

"Really?"

"She's in the nursing program so she can help support her firefighter boyfriend. Isn't that cute?"

"She's nice to everyone but me and cute when she's with Kunimi, then."

She *was* Yuuma Kunimi's girlfriend.

"Oh, don't tell her I called her cute," Ikumi said.

"Don't worry—we'll likely never see each other again."

Even if they spotted each other around campus, he certainly didn't plan to initiate contact. Saki likely shared that reluctance.

"Why'd you choose the nursing school, Akagi?"

"Nurses help those in need."

Where most people would be evasive or noncommittal, Ikumi was startlingly candid about her motivation. And if she was answering like that, Sakuta couldn't exactly joke around, either.

But that suited his purposes. He was getting sick of tiptoeing around each other.

"So that's why you believed the dreaming hashtag and did the whole hero thing? While in a nurse costume?"

He maintained the exact same tone, but that was a huge leap to make.

"I don't always wear that costume! I was just dressed for a Halloween event with the junior high kids in the volunteer classroom."

Ikumi didn't seem rattled by his suddenly getting to the heart of the matter. Maybe slightly embarrassed that he'd seen her in that outfit.

"You save people a lot, then?"

She'd only denied the dressing-up part.

"Is that bad?"

No deflections. She just wanted to know what he thought.

"I had you down as someone who didn't believe in the occult."

At least in junior high, she hadn't believed in Adolescence Syndrome. She'd been one of many students who'd refused to hear his pleas.

"……"

And she knew that. Ikumi pursed her lips, as if searching for the right thing to say.

"Azusagawa…," she began, her lips trembling.

Guessing where that was going, he cut her off. "Don't say sorry. I won't know how to react."

It was all in the past. She had nothing to apologize for. Dredging up that guilt now would just be a headache.

"Then I won't," she said, relaxing.

"So what did you want from me?"

She'd probably accomplished her main goal already. He figured she was here to suss out what he thought about yesterday.

"I imagine you won't want to come, but we're doing a class reunion at the end of the month."

This, he had not anticipated.

"……"

And since Akagi was bringing it up, she didn't mean elementary or high school.

"A junior high one," she added softly.

"Yeah, I'm not interested."

He'd meant to answer normally, but his voice sounded awfully far-away. Part of him was still dragging along some baggage. He laughed at himself.

"Since we ran into each other, I figured I'd at least pass on the flyer," Ikumi said.

She stepped closer and handed over a folded piece of paper. It seemed like a hassle to refuse, so he took it off her hands. Inside were the details for the reunion.

Sunday, November 27. Four PM. A shop near Yamashita Park.

"Don't worry about me. You go have fun."

"I'm probably not going, either."

"Why not?"

He didn't really want to know. Conversational etiquette just demanded he ask.

"Girls with boyfriends'll be boasting about them."

"'My boyfriend's hot *and* he's at a good school'?"

"'When will *you* find someone, Ikumi?'"

"Is that what reunions are like?"

He'd never had a reason to attend one, so he had no firsthand experience. He didn't feel like he was missing out, either.

"They're fun if you've got stuff to brag about."

That remark was definitely pointed his way.

"Well, I *am* dating Mai."

"If you showed up at the reunion, you'd silence everyone."

"But that's not why I'm going out with her."

"Then why are you?"

"So we can be happy together."

This was the truth, phrased as a joke. The intent was to make her laugh.

"......"

Ikumi didn't laugh. She just blinked in surprise. Then flushed slightly and fanned herself.

"Stop, I can't handle the residual embarrassment!"

"You got nothing?"

"Nothing what?"

"To brag about."

"Good question."

She managed an evasive smile. She could have just gone for the same white lie, but she didn't.

He was starting to feel like there was a distinct reason why she didn't want to go. Maybe a big fight with someone he didn't know about, someone she didn't want to run into again.

Ikumi's eyes flicked to the clock.

"I'd better leave."

He didn't ask if she had places to go. The look on her face alone told him what this was.

Her eyes caught his computer screen and the list of hashtag search results on it.

So he knew she was headed out again to save someone from misfortune, guided by the hashtag dreaming posts.

"Bye," she said, shouldering her backpack.

As she headed to the door, Sakuta called, "Don't save too many."

She stopped and half turned, asking, "Why not?"

"Sometimes changing the future can lead to a worse outcome."

Possibly the worst one. He was all too aware of that.

"I know. I'll be careful."

Ikumi smiled and left the lab.

Sakuta reached for his mouse.

"She doesn't get it at *all*."

He clicked the shutdown button.

He had a cram school class to teach and couldn't be fussing over other people's problems. Sakuta had his own life to lead.

2

When Sakuta got to the cram school, he found Rio in the free space outside the faculty area. She was already wearing her teacher's jacket—a blazer that looked a lot like a white lab coat.

She was talking to a boy in a Minegahara uniform. A pretty tall one, at least a head taller than she was. The dots connected.

"The basketball kid Kunimi mentioned."

Two years younger than them, a second-year player.

Rio was explaining how to solve a problem, and he was listening intently.

"You calculate the momentum first…"

She started writing a formula in a notebook on the table. She leaned forward to do so, which put her closer to the student. That must have gotten to him, because he leaned back, keeping his distance.

The way he spoke was a bit tense—standard enough for a boy talking to a girl. But it felt like there was a bit more going on. His eyes were less on the pen running across the page than Rio's expression.

"Then you just follow the formula. Give it a try."

Rio looked up as she finished writing. Her eyes met the boy's, and he quickly turned his gaze toward the vending machine.

Ah, youth. That made it pretty hard to miss.

"Are you listening?" Rio asked.

"I'm listening."

A low, steady voice.

"You understand?"

"I do not."

"Because you weren't listening?"

"Sorry."

As Sakuta watched this, both noticed him looking.

"Um, thank you. I'll give it another try," the tall boy said, closing the notebook before heading off to a self-study room.

"Ask again if you get stuck," Rio called.

"Will do," he said, turning back and bowing. This time the door closed behind him.

"Kunimi's kohai?"

"Seems like."

"He got a name?"

"Toranosuke Kasai."

Her eyes told him that she was wondering why he'd asked.

"Just thought it could get interesting."

"......?"

Rio didn't seem to catch his drift. That wasn't like her. But she did seem like the type to be oblivious to this kind of attention. It was much easier to see from the outside.

"I've got a class to prep."

"Oh, wait, Futaba..."

"What?"

"You heard of hashtag dreaming?"

"Of course."

"It really is a thing."

Maybe it was something people naturally stumbled across by virtue of using a phone regularly.

"Is this Touko Kirishima related?"

"Akagi was using that hashtag to play hero."

Probably still was. Given the way she'd acted when she left, Sakuta was confident she was on her way to save someone else.

"What for?"

"Just can't leave well enough alone, I guess. She started a volunteer club, too. That girl's big on helping people."

"Was she like that back in the day?"

"I think she was, like, class president or on the student council?"

He really didn't remember.

There were thirty kids in a class, and you could easily go the whole year without speaking to some of them. To Sakuta, that's all Ikumi Akagi had been.

"But from what you've said, this isn't actually her Adolescence Syndrome. Wasn't that the whole premise here?"

"That it was."

Ikumi was just using a hashtag to help people. But the posts tagged #dreaming were all being independently posted by total strangers.

She'd seen one of those and used it to help save the little girl from the pumpkin lantern. That was all.

No part of that gave any hint as to what Ikumi's own Adolescence Syndrome might be. The matter resolved itself without anything like that getting involved.

"Futaba, what's your take on it?"

"If it's not causing problems for her, you should let it be."

Rio had a point there.

"If she's being a hero and running a volunteer group, then I don't see how she's suffering from Adolescence Syndrome."

"That's the thing."

Ikumi seemed untroubled.

In every case of Adolescence Syndrome Sakuta had previously encountered, the afflicted had been driven into a corner. There were usually strong emotions involved.

But he didn't sense anything like that coming from Ikumi.

The only exception had been Uzuki's case. No dramatic changes, just a gradual shift. Before she knew it, she was different.

"Nice, huh? Having someone besides you playing hero."

Rio slapped his shoulder with her file, like she was congratulating him on a job well done. Then she headed into a study pod.

"It is high time I left adolescence behind," Sakuta muttered.

He went into the locker room to change.

After an overview of the midterms, he spent a good fifteen minutes teaching his students how to solve quadratic functions.

"Sakuta-sensei, we need a break! I'm totally fried!" Kento Yamada wailed, collapsing onto the desk. His uniform jacket was slung over the back of his chair—it was from Minegahara, the same place Sakuta had gone.

His other student, Juri Yoshiwa, wore the same uniform except it was the girls' version.

The two of them were seated at a long table built for three. An empty seat between them. There was a whiteboard on the wall across from them, and that was Sakuta's default position. Sometimes he drew on the board; sometimes he taught while hovering over their notebooks.

He'd finished explaining how to solve things, and they were tackling practice problems. Kento's focus had run out before he managed to get through them all.

"Yamada, this class lasts another half hour."

Cram school classes were a full eighty minutes.

"That's an eternity!"

Compared with the length of high school classes, it certainly was pretty long. But from a teaching perspective, it went by surprisingly quick.

"It's a teacher's job to keep their students motivated," Kento snarked, chin on the table.

Sakuta glanced at Juri, who'd been studiously working on the problems—and she was stifling a yawn. Not as blatant as Kento, but her focus was clearly flagging, too.

"Okay, we'll take five."

"Yes!"

Sakuta was still getting paid for it, which made him feel a bit guilty. But if his students wanted a break, who was he to argue? Still, five minutes in silence would put them both to sleep.

"You heard of this hashtag dreaming thing?" he asked.

"Do you believe that stuff, Sakuta-sensei? That's bad news."

"Not as bad as your midterm scores, Yamada."

He'd been shown answer sheets with a big ole *30* at the top of them, worse than he'd feared. Since he was tutoring the kid, Sakuta would've liked it if he got good grades.

"I had a dream come true," Juri said, breaking her silence. "A month ago, I dreamed I'd score a winning point with a service ace."

She meant in a beach volleyball match. Juri was on a Hiratsuka team. The reason she still sported a healthy tan in November was easily explained by her sport of choice.

"I posted about it with the hashtag, and then it came true in the match last Sunday."

"But you also practiced like hell before it and landed exactly the serve you wanted, right?" Kento said. He was still flat on the desk, sounding bored.

"……"

Juri took a good long look at him. Perhaps she hadn't expected it from him.

"Trust yourself, not this supernatural crap," Kento said, totally oblivious.

"You took what I said way too seriously," she said, already back to her usual self. She wasn't looking in his direction anymore.

"Th-that wasn't on purpose!"

Kento shot up in open denial. It was apparent he felt called out. Meanwhile, Juri's eyes were locked on Sakuta.

"Then you're just being creepy."

"Creepy?! That's so not fair!"

"Never said I was," she snapped, before he could argue further.

There wasn't much he could say to that.

His lips flapped for a minute, and then he looked around for help.

"Let's keep it down. Futaba-sensei's teaching next door, and I don't want her telling me off again."

No sooner had the words left Sakuta's mouth than there was a knock on the cubicle wall.

"See? She's here."

He turned to the entrance, ready to get an earful.

But the face peering around the partition was not grumpy Rio.

It was a girl in a Minegahara uniform.

One he'd spoken to once before.

Her name was Sara Himeji. She bobbed her head, wavy hair swaying.

"Sorry, is this a good time? Seemed like you were just chatting."

"Huh? Himeji?"

Kento swung around to stare, his voice cracking.

"Funny seeing you out of school," Sara said with a giggle, waving.

Kento's grin got real sloppy. It was obvious he was too embarrassed to wave back and unsure what else to do with himself.

"……"

Juri glanced once at the two of them, then looked away.

"What brings you here, Himeji?" Sakuta asked.

She wasn't his student, so he figured she wasn't here for him.

"Mind if I sit in on one of your classes, Azusagawa-sensei?"

"Like I said, if you actually want to understand the math, Futaba-sensei's a better choice."

"But if I want to pass my tests, you are," she said, winking at him.

"That's certainly my intent, but my confidence has been badly shaken."

"How so?" she asked, long lashes fluttering.

"Yamada here got a thirty."

"Sakuta-sensei! That's private information!"

"What an idiot," Juri said with her chin in her hand.

"Hey!" Kento said, but before he could protest further, Sara sat down in the vacant middle seat.

"Oh, it is a thirty!" she said, examining his answer sheet. That shut Kento up quick.

He turned forward, back perfectly straight.

Boys were *so* obvious.

And the finishing blow—

"Lemme share your textbook," Sara said, her shoulder bumping his.

"Mine?"

"We're classmates!"

"Right…"

He was doing his absolute best to act like this didn't get to him, and

Sakuta had to try equally hard not to laugh. But he decided it was best not to leak any other personal information, so he called an end to the break and resumed his lesson.

3

The class started at seven and wrapped up exactly eighty minutes later, at 8:20 PM. Sakuta erased the formulas on the whiteboard and left the learning room.

Kento always left his chair askew, but this time Sara had straightened them all out.

He spent ten minutes logging what he'd taught today in the teacher's room. The principal caught him and asked about Sara, which took about five minutes. Then he hit the locker room to change, saw Rio at her desk and said, "Bye," and was out the door twenty minutes after classes ended, at 8:40.

He should make it home before nine.

Mai was coming over to cook dinner, so the sooner he could get home the better.

The elevator arrived, and he stepped on board, hitting the button for the ground floor.

"Oh, wait!"

Sara slipped through the doors as they started to close.

"Safe!" she exclaimed.

"I'm afraid you're out," he said. He'd reached for the OPEN button but retracted his hand at the last second.

The doors closed, and the elevator began to descend.

"Azusagawa-sensei is far too long. Can I call you Sakuta-sensei like Yamada does?"

"He really doesn't make that seem like a term of respect."

Kento's attitude was more like he was talking to a friend.

"Then I'll just call you Teach!" she said with a giggle.

"How'd I get to be so approachable?"

"You don't seem like a teacher. In a good way!"

"If you say so."

The elevator reached the ground floor.

Sakuta followed Sara out. Both turned toward the station.

"You take the train from here, Himeji?"

"I live over by Kataseyama, so my mom picks me up. I should hear from her any minute."

Sara pulled her phone out of the pocket on her satchel. As she did, the hand towel in the same pocket fell out.

"You dropped something," he said, kneeling to grab it.

"Oh, I got it," Sara said, hastily bending over to do the same.

By the time he realized the threat, it was too late.

There was a loud clunk that echoed through his skull. They'd both bent down and thumped their heads together, hard.

"Owww…," she said, clutching it with both hands.

There was a throbbing pain in his forehead, too.

"You okay, Teach? My head's like a rock!"

"It feels like mine split in two."

"Oh no! Let me take a look!"

She put her hands on his shoulders, stretching as high as she could. This was a pose that could easily be misconstrued.

"You're totally fine," she huffed, then laughed.

"Here," he said, handing her the towel.

"Thanks. Oh, it's my mom."

Her phone had started ringing, and she picked up.

"Mm, I'm outside. Be right there," she said. Then she looked at him. "Okay, Teach, gotta run!"

She bobbed her head and ran off toward the roundabout, leaving him with an aching head.

"She was right about the rock thing…"

He gingerly prodded it and found a lump forming.

Alone again, Sakuta headed home, walking a bit faster than usual. The fall air was chilly, so a speed that worked up a sweat felt pretty good.

He crossed the bridge over the Sakai River, waited at a light, and then went up the gentle slope beyond. Once past the park, he was almost home.

He caught his breath before heading in.

Inside the building doors, he checked the mailbox, then took the elevator to the fifth floor.

He turned the key in the lock and heard voices from within.

"I'm home," he called, opening the door.

There were more shoes than usual in the entrance. There was almost nowhere left to stand. He managed to get his sneakers off, and a girl in an apron came out to see him.

"Welcome home! Do you want dinner? A bath? Orrrrr…"

"What are you doing, Zukki?" he asked, interrupting her clichéd routine.

It was Uzuki Hirokawa, in the flesh, a ladle in one hand.

"I heard they were making curry, and I simply could not stay away!"

A fitting reason for Uzuki. He couldn't exactly call it a good one, but if he argued the point, he'd likely be stuck at the door for quite a while. No thanks. This was *his* house.

"Zukki, you're on the cusp right now. You don't want a media circus," he said, moving down the hall.

"If anyone takes pictures of this, the headlines will just be 'Uzuki Hirokawa's Curry Night'!"

"Maybe that'll net you a curry commercial."

With that, he poked his head in the living room.

"I'm back."

"Welcome home, Sakuta."

Mai was standing in the kitchen. She wore high-waisted wide-leg pants and a sweater that was just on the brink of exposing her shoulders. On top of that was an apron.

Two more voices greeted him, and he turned to find Kaede and Nodoka sitting in front of the TV, only their heads looking his way. The screen was showing a *tokusatsu* hero show that aired on Sunday mornings. A familiar-looking villainous minion was cackling on-screen. One of Sweet Bullet's many members, Hotaru Okazaki.

Nodoka must have brought the recording to share with Kaede.

"Quite the homecoming, huh?!" Uzuki cried, slapping his shoulder enthusiastically.

He glanced around the crowd.

"Sure are a lot of you," he said. This was his honest impression.

"You're the last arrival, so go wash your hands and take a seat."

"Aww. I thought I'd get to spend some time with you, Mai."

But he stumped off to the washroom, rinsed his hands, and gargled.

"And you will——when we eat," Mai quipped.

He took her at her word and sat down at the table.

"Here," Mai said, putting an oblong plate of curry in front of him.

It was very runny.

More of a soup curry.

The scent of the spices was tantalizing.

It consisted of pretty basic ingredients. Just chicken and fried veggies—potatoes, eggplant, and zucchini.

"Everyone helped chop the veggies," Mai said, taking off her apron and sitting down across from him. She kept her promise to stay with him as he ate.

He scooped up a lump of potato. It was a decidedly square piece.

"Toyohama handled the potatoes, I see."

"Don't grumble. Eat."

"That doesn't even count as a complaint."

Whatever the shape might be, the hot potato matched the spiciness of the soup perfectly. Even Nodoka's handiwork couldn't ruin that.

His next spoonful of soup featured the eggplant. It was not well chopped, just roughly quartered. But it had absorbed some oil while frying, and that made it glisten appetizingly.

"Kaede did the eggplant?"

"Will you shut up and eat?"

"I haven't said a bad word yet!"

There was an old saying about not letting your wife eat autumn eggplant, and he could see why they wouldn't wanna share.

The last vegetable sampled was the zucchini. The green definitely gave the brown soup some much needed color.

"Hirokawa did the zucchini? Oh, because you're Zukki?"

"Bingo!"

Uzuki was clapping enthusiastically.

After he savored the flavors of the vegetables, it was finally time for the chicken. The thigh meat had been simmering for a long time to achieve maximum tenderness, and he could easily split it apart with his spoon. He filled the split with soup, and the tingle of the spices and the umami of the meat filled his mouth with delight. It was hard not to wolf it down.

"Mai, this is amazing."

"Glad to hear it."

She had her cheek cupped in her hand, watching him eat with a smile.

"My Mai is adorable again today," he said.

If it had just been the two of them, this would be perfect. But there were far too many interlopers.

"Oh! I brought something for you," Uzuki said, already interrupting.

She started rummaging around in her bag. "Mm? Where'd they go!" She ended up dumping the bag out.

"There they are!"

She came up with two slips of paper, which she brought to the dining room table.

"We're doing a concert next Monday at the school festival. You should come, too, Mai!"

Uzuki put the slips of paper down. They were unmistakably concert tickets.

"Which school festival?"

"Ours," Nodoka said, deep into the couch's cushions. She treated this place like it was her house.

Peering closer at the tickets, he saw that they did bear the name of their college.

"Sweet Bullet is a special guest at this year's festival!" Uzuki said, throwing up a peace sign.

"Making your triumphant return already?"

Uzuki had—of her own accord—dropped out of college a week ago. Naturally, this must have been arranged before that happened, and her sudden withdrawal probably horrified a number of people involved.

"Why don't you know about this?" Kaede asked.

"Nobody told me."

"I thought Uzuki had."

"I thought *I* had!"

Nobody bought Uzuki's excuse. It was more of an admission of guilt.

"Well, I'll certainly take the tickets, but…Mai, are you working?"

That was the first and greatest hurdle.

"I left that day open so the two of us could make the festival rounds."

"First I've heard of it."

"I held my tongue in case a last-minute job came in, forced me to back out, and then left me stuck doing whatever you dream up as payback. How's your schedule Monday?"

"Kaede, can you take my shift at the restaurant?"

"Can't. Komi and I are hitting the concert."

She proudly flourished her pair of tickets. These were obviously also a gift.

"Guess that leaves Koga."

"Should I ask her for you?" Kaede reached for her phone.

"Please."

"Just a sec."

Kaede started tapping her screen. She was probably messaging Tomoe that very instant.

"She's writing back!"

"She would be fast."

Tomoe was a very modern high school girl, and her phone was her best friend.

"She's got a hankering for the cream puffs from the shop by the station."

"Tell her I'll buy her ten."

"She already added 'One is plenty.'"

She'd known exactly what he'd say. That was Laplace's demon for you.

"Can't wait to have a campus date with you, Mai."

"At least mention the concert!" Nodoka snapped, vaulting to her feet. "Mai, Uzuki and I are heading back first. We'll run the bath."

"Oh? Thanks."

The little hand was almost at ten. "Bye!" Nodoka waved and headed for the door.

"Kaede! Sakuta! Thanks for having me! Mai, you still will be."

Uzuki went after her. Sakuta got up to see them out.

"Zukki. You're staying at Mai's place?" he asked as she put her shoes on.

"Mwa-ha-ha!"

He got a mysterious chortle in return. No doubt she was boasting.

"This bath is the perfect excuse to see how Nodoka's grown!"

"I'm not bathing *with* you, Uzuki."

With that curt remark, Nodoka was out the door.

"Aww! We gotta share!"

Uzuki threw her arms around Nodoka's back.

"Oh, Kaede, see you later!" she yelled, waving through the closing door.

"Uh, right!" Kaede managed to wave just before the door fully shut.

With their exit, the house felt quiet again.

Normalcy had been restored.

He locked the door and headed back to the living room.

Mai was already clearing the table.

"Mai, I'll do that."

"Can you make some coffee instead?"

"Got it. You want any, Kaede?"

"Nah, I'm gonna take a bath."

With that, she disappeared into her room. She soon came out carrying her pajamas.

"Oh, Kaede."

"Yes?"

"Gonna borrow your laptop later."

"Don't use it for anything weird."

"Just looking some stuff up."

At this point, she was undoubtedly far better with computers than he was. The whole remote-learning thing had turned it into a useful tool—after all, her school was *on* the computer.

"That's fine, then," she said, and she vanished into the washroom.

The door shut behind her, and he heard the lock turn. She was at an age where these things mattered.

"Looking up the dreaming hashtag?" Mai asked, drying her hands. The dishes were taken care of. He'd told her about last night—and the mixer—over lunch at school.

"Can't hurt to read a few more."

He picked up two mugs of coffee and followed her out of the kitchen. The mugs were part of a set with animal pictures on them. Mai's was the bunny, and Sakuta's was a tanuki. She'd picked that for him on the grounds that their eyes looked alike.

There were two other mugs from that set on the shelf. The panda belonged to Kaede, and the lion was Nodoka's. They'd bought all four in the spring when they went to see the pandas at the zoo together.

He put the bunny and tanuki mugs down on the dining room table, then took a seat on the couch in front of the TV. Kaede's laptop was on the coffee table, and he opened the lid.

As he pressed the power button, Mai said, "Oh, Sakuta, take this."

She handed him a blue envelope.

"Kaede said it came today."

It was addressed to Sakuta Azusagawa. The neat handwriting alone told him who'd sent it. For one thing, nobody else sent him letters.

He opened it up, took out the missive within, and unfolded it.

> *Has autumn arrived for you yet?*
>
> *We're still stuck in summer.*
>
> *I've included a photo to show you Shouko. See what I did there?*

Nice and short.

"Photo?"

"In there."

Mai picked up the envelope he'd dropped on the table and took out the picture.

"Here," she said, holding it up for him.

Mountainous clouds against the blue of the sky. The clear waters of the southern seas too beautiful to look real. Shouko was standing barefoot on soft sands, smiling. She had the hem of her T-shirt knotted on one hip, healthy legs peeping from below short culottes. She had her hands up, framing a heart-shaped rock out in the surf.

Without question, quite a lot of work had gone into placing the camera and the angle of the shot to make it look like that. And she'd written *I love you!* next to the heart.

"Shouko's becoming more and more like the bigger one."

"That she is."

The way she acted was one thing, but she'd also grown quite a bit since her move to Okinawa. Her face was shifting from little Makinohara to the older Shouko. When they'd met, she was in her first year of junior high, but now she was in her third. How time flew. And time naturally led to growth—and knowing she *had* that time gave him warm fuzzies.

"I can't let my guard down," Mai said.

She put the photo down and reached for the coffee mug on the dining room table.

"Mm?" he said, not sure what she meant. This earned him a cross look.

"She'll turn into your first love before long."

In the photo, she was already starting to look like her.

"Oh."

He nodded.

"Thrilled?" Mai asked, settling down next to him on the couch.

"Sure. I mean, this spring, she'll be in high school. Like she dreamed about."

The odds had been against her surviving junior high.

Despite the doctor's warnings, she'd lived and was now on the cusp of high school. That meant more for her than Sakuta's own higher education—he'd been *born* with a healthy body.

Shouko's life now had a future. She was living that out.

How could he not be thrilled?

"Now I sound like the bad guy…" Mai stuck out her lower lip, then took a sip from the mug in her hands. "You put in too much. It's really bitter," she grumbled.

That somehow made him laugh. They could bicker like this because they had each other. And savoring that modest pleasure, Sakuta put the letter and photo back in the envelope. By this time, the laptop had finished booting up, so he turned his attention to the screen.

To search #dreaming.

He clicked the tag and got a whole stream of posts.

He skimmed them but didn't spot anything odd. Most were just vague memories of dreams. Highly unrealistic, few that formed any sort of story. Just accounts of what they'd dreamed the night before.

But buried in that morass, he found a few with clear dates and times, set apart from the rest by weirdly vivid details.

The specificity itself felt odd.

Most dreams didn't come with a time stamp.

Sakuta had only experienced that in one dream—the time he got caught up in Tomoe's future simulation. Which he'd believed was real…

Perhaps this was what Ikumi had latched on to.

"Sakuta, how do you feel about your old classmates now?"

Mai had her legs crossed on the couch and was resting the coffee mug on her knee.

"Now…?"

He didn't exactly have an answer ready off the cuff.

"You don't really talk about junior high," she said.

"I guess I don't feel much of anything."

At some point, he'd just stopped thinking about that stuff entirely. So he meant what he said. He had no doubts at all.

"It just led to too much."

"Like meeting your first love."

Poking him while acting all innocent.

"And encountering a wild bunny girl."

"High time you forgot that."

"And just…a lot happened."

"Yeah."

"Going to Minegahara, making friends with Kunimi and Futaba. Then you were there, and Kaede got better…so somewhere along the way it just stopped bothering me."

It wasn't like he'd forgotten everything that went down. No one there had understood him, and that left him ostracized and deeply depressed—that kind of thing sticks with you.

But afterward? He'd met people who mattered. Gained more than he'd lost. He didn't have any reason to stay hung up on the past.

New bonds and time spent with the people he cared about gradually made the darkness of those memories fade. All kinds of new experiences mingled with the old ones, turning them to shades of gray.

"So you've forgiven Ikumi Akagi for her part in it?"

"Forgive…?"

He'd never held anything against her in particular.

All he had to do was say that.

Yet the words wouldn't quite come out.

"……"

He'd found a tiny little sore spot deep down inside. Like the past had left a splinter slumbering at the bottom of his heart.

"……"

When Sakuta fell silent, Mai said nothing more. She just leaned her shoulder against his, reminding him that she was here with him. Her touch gave him comfort.

"Acceptance is hard," she said.

"For you, too?"

"I struggle *every* time you make friends with another girl."

She made that sound like a joke, but one glance in her direction made it clear she meant it. The way she put it was gentle, but her warning was sharp as any nail.

"I'll try to be more careful."

"Not getting my hopes up."

"Aww."

"If you're that confident, then promise you'll do a thing for me for each new girl you add."

"Like what?"

"I know this one famous actress makes her husband build her a new house every time he breaks a promise."

"Maybe I should go apprentice myself to a carpenter."

"Or maybe just don't cheat?"

She leaned on him harder.

"And she's not having him build them himself."

Sakuta had been well aware.

"Well, I'm not gonna cheat, so there's no problem here."

"Yet your thoughts are entirely on this Ikumi Akagi." With that bit of spite, Mai sat back upright. "Or should I say Touko Kirishima?"

The scales had probably leaned toward Ikumi since Halloween.

"I dunno. Akagi's just on my mind."

"Mm-hmm."

"Not like that."

"Then like what?"

Three reasons.

"Touko Kirishima said Akagi had Adolescence Syndrome, too."

That was the first.

"Then there was the Akagi I met in that other potential world."

This was the second. In that world, Akagi and Sakuta had both gone to Minegahara. If he hadn't seen her there, when she spoke to him at the college entrance ceremony, he probably wouldn't have recognized her as an old classmate and definitely wouldn't have known her name.

"And I guess her being in the same junior high is a factor."

The third reason was the least concrete. It was just a fact; there was no real connection between them because of it. None at all. Yet despite this, if they hadn't gone to the same school, he was sure he'd never have taken an interest in Ikumi at all. Even if Touko Kirishima had pointed her out as having Adolescence Syndrome, he wouldn't have cared.

It was the least significant reason, yet also the thing that refused to leave him alone.

They'd gone to the same junior high.

Their relationship was no more and no less than what that phrase implied.

But looked at another way, perhaps that meant their roots were entwined.

Sakuta had gone to public elementary and junior high schools, so his first glimpses of the world at large came from those places and their satellites.

Most kids who grew up in that area had played in the same parks, begged their parents for candy at the same supermarket, and been yelled at by the same scary old man who lived on the corner.

These days, Fujisawa had become his neighborhood of choice, but the streets of the Yokohama suburb he'd grown up in would always be a part of him. Even if they were all too typical and devoid of distinguishing features.

It was still where he came from.

And Ikumi had been a part of that place. She'd been there all fifteen years he was. That number still represented the vast majority of his time alive.

Perhaps that was why going to the same junior high meant more than the words implied, more than going to the same high school or college did.

"I guess I can't quite call her a stranger."

That's what it felt like. They'd talked a lot about where they'd come from at the mixer, too. "I know that junior high!" or "I've been to the shop by that station!" Shared memories of local neighborhoods made them all feel closer together.

"Maybe you're right, Sakuta. I wouldn't know—I really don't remember anyone from back then."

Mai's child acting career had been her priority during those years. She'd mentioned barely ever actually going to school.

"I wonder if she feels the same way about you?"

"Yeah…"

He started to reject the idea. His role in junior high had hardly been typical. But even if her perspective was different, she *had* been there. In that neighborhood, in that school, in that class.

If Mai hadn't pointed it out, it might never have occurred to him.

When Kaede was getting bullied, when Sakuta started yelling about Adolescence Syndrome…what had his classmates thought? What had they made of it?

In his mind, it had all been about him. He'd never stopped to wonder how anyone else felt. That seemed so trivial compared with what he'd been going through.

He'd fully believed he was the only miserable one.

But that may not have been true. All thirty or so of his classmates had feelings of their own. And in that moment—they'd likely not been amused or entertained.

The mood in the room had been bleak as hell.

Kaede's friend Kotomi Kano had told him about it once. After they moved away, there'd been a witch hunt, targeting the girls who'd been mean to Kaede. They'd all wound up dropping out and moving away.

The class had banished evil and then closed the door on the matter.

Then they finished out their junior high years, acting like it was all forgotten.

Sakuta's classmates hadn't even waited that long. They'd graduated and left, like third-year students do.

He had no idea what they'd gotten up to at their respective high schools. Three years might have been enough for some of them to cleanse their emotions. Had most of them put Sakuta out of their minds entirely? He figured they had.

Ikumi Akagi alone had run into him again.

And honestly, he couldn't imagine what that had been like.

But he presumed it had meant something.

Even Sakuta still registered her as a junior high classmate. She was significant enough to earn a label.

And that label had existed before his girlfriend, Mai, before his friends Yuuma and Rio, and before his first love, Shouko.

He had a sort of latent affinity with her. Perhaps a lingering resentment that just resembled affinity.

And Mai's question had helped him finally start to see why he couldn't get her out of his mind.

"I dunno if meeting you again has anything to do with what she's doing," Mai said. She gazed into her mug as if staring down memory lane. "But the two of us know a few things."

"We do."

He knew exactly what she meant.

"Just how hard and painful changing the future can be. If that's for someone who matters, I won't—can't—say not to."

Doing so would go against what the two of them had done. It would be an insult to everything that girl smiling in the Okinawa sun had been through.

"But, Mai…you're against these heroics."

"We know all too well that one person's happiness is another's misfortune."

"Yeah."

All those tears and suffering. Struggling, fighting, scrambling—for nothing. And finally getting their hands on what they had now.

And that was why they didn't need to spell it out. Their feelings were linked.

Ikumi's choices weren't wrong. Saving the Little Red Riding kid from the falling lantern was a good thing. But there was no telling what might be in store for that kid in a few days or even years because she'd avoided that fate.

There was no telling what Ikumi's actions might cause.

Saving that kid changed the future. And no one could be sure the outcome wouldn't be far worse.

"But that makes me sound like a villain trying to thwart the hero's deeds."

Mai's eyes turned to the TV screen. It was still playing that *tokusatsu* hero show. Hotaru Okazaki had shown up as a new minion of evil and was siccing a horrible monster on the heroes.

"Then we'd better make like villains and start an evil society."

Mai had given him the motivation to reach for the laptop again. It was still showing that social media site. He picked a username and password and made an account. He chose a picture of Nasuno yawning for the profile icon.

"Appointing you leader, Nasuno," Sakuta said.

She just meowed sleepily.

4

November 6—the day of the school festival—arrived too fast for him to grow impatient.

In that time, Sakuta only went to college once: Wednesday, November 2. The only thing of note was asking Miori about her mixer.

"Were the guys actually hot, then?"

"On the way to the shop, a Halloween parade cut me off, and I lost track of Manami. So I never actually found out!"

"You should pay more attention," Sakuta said, like he hadn't done the same thing.

Miori also didn't carry a phone.

"I was all down for the meat, at least. There was supposedly a lot of it."

The day after—the third—the college was closed for a holiday. On the fourth, all classes were suspended in the name of festival prep.

The festival itself started on the fifth, but he spent that working.

So when he finally made it back to campus, the festival was in full swing. A very different vibe.

Through the heavily decorated gate, the path through the gingkoes was jam-packed with people and stalls lined both sides.

People here to have fun, students running the booths, voices calling out, mascot characters carrying signs around—it was immediately apparent that there were far more people here than during the usual morning rush.

Very much a festival crowd.

Just getting down that path took a while.

The Sweet Bullet concert was on the outdoor stage—the festival's main venue.

Encore included, they performed seven songs. Six were Sweet Bullet originals. The last was a famous Touko Kirishima number—"Social World," the song Uzuki had covered for the commercial.

The student MC got a bit carried away and started ad-libbing, taking questions from the crowd, and calling for an encore they hadn't planned, but the girls all rolled with it and gave the crowd what they wanted.

When it was over, Sakuta poked his head in the classroom that served as their greenroom and found Ranko Nakagou grumbling, "Who does that MC think he is?!"

And the others were laughing.

The Sweet Bullet members only got a short break; then they had to move to the auditorium. There was a (male) beauty contest, and they'd been asked to hand out bouquets and congratulate the victors.

And since the concert had run long, they didn't even get time to eat. They left the greenroom, saddling Sakuta with a shopping list.

On it were requests from each of them. *Yakisoba*, bubble tea, *takoyaki*, chocolate-covered bananas, and tacos.

He was under strict orders to have that all back here before their presenter job was done.

To that end, he started making the rounds of the stalls and was currently in line at the taco stand. Mai was with him, holding the *yakisoba*.

Kaede and her friend Kotomi Kano had been tasked with acquiring bubble tea and chocolate bananas. They were lined up in front of some other stall.

"So much bigger than high school culture festivals."

Mai had a cap pulled down low but was looking around with evident curiosity. She was wearing a hoodie and jeans with sneakers—a tomboyish streetwear look.

Nothing like what *the* Mai Sakurajima wore in all the magazines or on TV, so not many people recognized her.

And for today alone, the campus was filled with sign-carrying mascots and colorfully costumed barkers.

An infinite number of distractions.

Anyone dressed normally wouldn't get a second glance.

In front of them was a big man in a judo outfit, and he was drawing all the attention. It was likely he was recruiting for the Judo Club.

He paid up and stepped aside.

"Welcome."

When Sakuta and Mai moved forward, they found a girl dressed as a nurse. It was the same costume design Ikumi had worn on Halloween.

When Sakuta saw who it was, he smiled. Saki Kamisato scowled back at him.

"I'll take some tacos," he said, undaunted.

"It's Azusagawa!"

"So it is!"

Behind Saki were the girls he'd met at the mixer, Chiharu and Asuka. They were all wearing the same nurse costume. And their eyes had turned toward Mai.

"The girls from the mixer," he said, figuring introductions were in order. "My girlfriend. You may have heard of her."

"Sh-she's real!" Chiharu gasped, hand over her mouth.

Mai smiled and bobbed her head.

"Did you see that? She bowed at me!"

Chiharu was now clutching Asuka's sleeve.

"That was for *me*," Asuka said.

"Order up." There were two male students behind the girls, bringing over the tacos: Takumi Fukuyama and Ryouhei Kodani, both from the mixer, and both on taco-creation duty.

"You're not dressing up?"

"Did you *want* to see me in a nurse outfit?"

"If I had a phone, I'd definitely have taken pics."

"Thank god you don't," Takumi grumbled, adding a squirt of salsa as a finishing touch.

Sakuta paid up, and Mai took half the tacos. That left both her hands full.

Sakuta took the rest of the tacos, and one more nurse emerged from the back of the stall. Ikumi.

"Everything good?" she asked, talking to Saki.

Then she spotted Sakuta and looked shifty.

His eyes were on her right arm. It was in a sling. That didn't seem like part of the costume. With her hand bandaged up like that, there was only so much she could do to help.

"Nice timing, Ikumi. Where's the extra salsa?" Asuka asked, turning around from the customer she'd been helping.

"In the cooler."

"Oh, Ikumi, we're low on mayo!" Chiharu called.

"I brought some out from the back," Ikumi said, putting down an industrial-sized container.

"Almost outta cabbage, too," Takumi added.

"The *yakisoba* stall said they'd share."

Even as Ikumi spoke, another college girl came in with two cabbages. "Cabbage delivery!" she said, handing one to Takumi and one to Ryouhei.

"Anything else low?"

"Should be good. You hit up the flea market, Ikumi," Saki said, speaking for everyone. "We've got enough help with these two," she added, pointing at the boys.

At that, Ikumi said, "Thanks for coming on such short notice," and headed off toward the flea market.

"What happened to Akagi's hand?" he asked Saki, watching Ikumi go.

"Tried to catch someone who stumbled on the station stairs."

"When?"

"Wednesday…?"

So right after she'd talked to Sakuta. Her hand had been fine then.

He wanted to ask more, but Saki's attention was already on the next customer. No time to stop and chat.

They moved away from the stall, not wanting to block the line.

"You can go after her," Mai said.

Meaning Ikumi, of course.

"I'll take these to the greenroom."

"I appreciate that Mai, but…"

He was glancing at his own hands. They were filled with the tacos they'd bought for themselves.

"What about the tacos?"

He couldn't exactly run after Ikumi carrying them.

"Go ahead," Mai said. Then she opened her mouth, like he should just push one in.

They *were* no bigger than a *gyoza*, so he went right ahead.

"Mm, that's good," she said in between bites.

"Then off I go," Sakuta said before scarfing down his own share. "You're right—it is good!"

Savoring the flavor, he headed after Ikumi.

Sakuta caught up with her just outside the campus flea market. She was resting on a bench in the shade, watching the flow of festival-goers.

He came up from behind and sat next to her, leaving a space between them.

"……"

She didn't visibly react. She must have expected him to follow. And to ask about the arm.

"Being injured is so boring," she said, eyes on the flea market. "They said they didn't need my help, either."

She mustered a rueful smile.

"Nobody wants to be the baddie and put someone injured to work."

"Oh, so they weren't just worried?" she said, laughing.

"It's easier if you look at it my way."

"That depends on the individual."

She might be rejecting the idea, but she seemed to have lightened up a little. His stare soon made her shift uncomfortably.

"When I showed Chiharu pictures of my Halloween costume, she said we absolutely had to use these for the taco stand." She plucked the hem of her apron with her uninjured hand. "Saki and I were against it."

"I'm here to ask about the arm, not the rockin' duds."

There'd been some distance between them at the stand, but seen up close, Ikumi's arm was in a sling, and the bandages were wound tight, keeping her wrist immobilized.

Her efforts to distract him thwarted, she tried to smile, eyes still on the flea market.

A fall breeze swept between them. Dry leaves danced in the air. Bright-yellow gingko leaves. Ikumi caught one and finally spoke.

"Think I'm an idiot for ignoring your warning?"

"That's your dominant hand, right? You getting by?"

It seemed like it would cause a lot of problems.

"I can see why you snagged Mai Sakurajima," she said with a laugh. She spun the leaf by the stem.

"I warned you, but you're dumber than you look, Akagi."

"Saki's taking notes for me, so I'm okay there. It looks bad, but it's just a sprain. It'll be healed in a week, and everyone I know is a budding nurse."

She was playing it off like a joke.

Their conversation wasn't quite adding up. She was intentionally not letting it. Not wanting to give him control.

"I hear you caught someone on the stairs?"

"……"

He tried asking outright, but she didn't answer and just played with the gingko leaf like it was a propeller.

"Azusagawa, do you remember what you wrote in your junior high graduation essay?"

When she finally did speak, her question came out of nowhere.

"I don't. I threw my graduation album out when we moved."

And he'd never once cracked it open. He'd put it in the trash when he was cleaning his room, and it had likely been incinerated somewhere and was now in its final resting place at the Minamihonmoku landfill. In a few years or decades, it would be part of some reclaimed land project.

"Well, I remember it."

Judging by the expression on her face, it wasn't a fond memory.

"……"

"I remember my own, and yours."

She spoke softly, the look on her face never changing.

"Pretty sure mine's worth forgetting. I doubt I wrote anything worthwhile."

"Oh, but you did."

"Yeah?"

"I mean, you wrote that you'd like to reach a place of kindness."

"……"

"Well? Have you, Azusagawa?"

Her eyes demanded an answer.

"Have you, Akagi?"

"……"

"Have you become the ideal self you imagined in junior high?"

"The prattle of a child. Not even worth laughing at."

"Too soon to act like you're all grown up, though. We're still students."

Neither Sakuta nor Ikumi was directly answering the other's questions. They weren't really talking. They were using lots of words but never managed to get on the same page.

"We're in college now. We can't still be kids."

"Is being a hero a grown-up's dream?"

"You'd rather Red Riding Hood got hurt?"

"I'd rather you didn't, Akagi."

"……"

Ikumi fell silent, staring down at her arm.

She was saying the right things.

And Sakuta wasn't saying anything wrong.

But they were at odds.

"I'll be more careful."

"But you're not gonna stop."

"……"

Ikumi didn't answer. Her silence *was* her answer. What was it that had made her so insistent on this? He couldn't figure it out. Was there something compelling her to act like this? Even if it was just out of the goodness of her heart, there had to be a deeper motive.

"Look over there," she said, pointing at a corner of the flea market. "The kids the volunteer group is teaching."

He followed where her beautifully pale finger was pointing and spotted some junior high kids. Two boys and a girl, working a stall.

"All of them were forced out of their schools."

They were talking. One boy was goofing off, the other laughed at him, and the girl was telling them both off. They all seemed like they were having fun; no one would've guessed they had to drop out just by looking at them. But that's how it went. All it took was one little thing, and you'd find your feet stuck to the ground one day, refusing to head into school. Sakuta knew how that went.

"They're selling the pottery they made together. Go check it out."

Sakuta glanced back at Ikumi and found her rising to her feet.

"I've got somewhere to be," she said before heading toward the ginkgo lane. He knew where she was bound.

He'd seen the tweet.

Weird dream. A boy tripped and fell by the clock tower. Cried a lot. During the school festival at the Kanazawa-hakkei campus. It was exactly three o'clock. This one of those prophecy dreams? #dreaming

Ikumi had probably seen it, too.

"No point heading to the clock tower," he said, before she got too far. "Nothing's gonna happen."

"……"

Ikumi stopped in her tracks, not turning around.

"The thing about the boy tripping and falling? I wrote that. Total fiction."

"……"

He could read nothing from her back.

Was she mad?

Had he pissed her off?

Maybe she was just frustrated.

Or did it go beyond that to outright disgust?

But when she was finally facing him again, it was none of the above.

"Well, good. We don't need any crying kids," she said, smiling.

"……"

It was his turn to fall silent.

Her reaction was exactly what you'd want from a hero.

No anger at being tricked.

Not mad at him.

Just relieved that nothing would happen and no one was gonna get hurt.

He was completely unprepared for that.

He'd hoped the trick would help him figure out where her heart lay, what was going on with her. Thought it might clue him in as to why she was helping people.

That's why he'd used the hashtag to bait her here.

But the result?

He had no clue what was going on in her head.

Ikumi was being the perfect hero.

And that was why it disturbed him.

What would lead someone to feel relieved that no one got hurt instead of getting angry after falling for a dirty trick?

"You really shouldn't do that," she said gently. Like she was reprimanding a naughty child. "We're in college now."

"Yeah. We're in college now," he echoed. He wondered how old you had to be before you stopped believing in heroes.

Then—

—the disturbance manifested.

"Don't copy me!" Ikumi said with a laugh—and then her body shook. "！"

She let out a little gasp, like she'd been elbowed in the ribs. Her lips tightened, and she knelt down.

"Akagi?" he called, moving closer.

He crouched down next to her, examining her face. Ikumi's cheeks were flushed. She was shaking, her free arm wrapped around herself. It seemed like each breath she took was more heated than the last.

"What's gotten into you?"

Some underlying condition? That was his first thought, but before he could ask, things got weirder.

"Sorry. I'm okay…" She tried gamely to smile at him…

…and the nurse cap she wore flew away.

But there was no wind.

It just *moved*.

Neither Ikumi nor Sakuta had touched it.

His mind flooded with question marks. His gaze followed it as the cap landed silently on the ground.

She'd had a hairpin holding the cap on and her hair up—and now it all came tumbling down. Nothing was touching her hair, but it was moving anyway. Pulling together, then falling apart, then gathered together by some invisible power once more. Even if there were a wind, it wouldn't move like this.

And that invisible force slipped in past her collar and down her neck, teased around her chest, then went lower still. He couldn't see it, but something was making wrinkles in her uniform. A dramatic tear ran down the white stockings below her skirt, and then a fist-sized hole tore open.

"……"

He had no words.

Sakuta hadn't laid a finger on Ikumi. He hadn't done anything.

Neither had she.

But some invisible force was at work.

"I swear, I'm fine," she gasped.

He had no clue what was going on, but her ragged breaths made her seem weirdly enticing.

Chapter
3
us, in backup memories

1

The medical office door opened, and Saki Kamisato came out, looking cross.

Once the unnatural attack on Ikumi subsided, Sakuta had carried her here. She hadn't fought him on that. Saki had brought a change of clothes from her things.

"How is she?"

"The doctor's examining her now."

"Ah."

"……"

Saki turned her eyes away from him and stared at the office door. There was no one else in the hall with them. MEDICAL OFFICE was written on a nearby white plate. Saki was still in her nurse costume, so it made the whole corridor feel like a hospital.

"Has Kunimi seen you dressed like that?" he asked when the silence got to be too much for him.

"Not yet," she said, clearly displeased. It was obvious she didn't want people to see her like this. Her every fiber was radiating that message.

"I think he'll like it. He likes bunny girls and miniskirt Santas, so I'm sure he'll go for nurses, too."

"What do you think Yuuma is?" Saki snapped, swinging around to glare at him.

"A friend who shares my enthusiasms."

"......"

Her scowl only deepened.

"What about you, Kamisato?"

"What about what?"

"What do you think about your friend?"

He glanced toward the door behind her. Was Ikumi still getting examined?

"Where's this coming from?"

"Akagi's earnest in a way that worries people, right? Entered nursing school to help people, big on the whole volunteer thing."

And following the hashtag to save people.

Saki nodded once at this, then thought for a long time.

"She's the definition of a good student," she said.

"Yeah."

That was an apt phrase.

"At first, I thought it was like a fashion statement."

"How so?"

"You know the type. People who get involved with one thing or another to make themselves look good. They're always part of some movement, or know some famous person, or just so busy because some event is coming up...but that's all just to cover how shallow they are. All the bragging and business cards aren't fooling anyone."

Sakuta couldn't stop himself from wincing. They'd both met one of those the other day.

"But Ikumi isn't like that. It's not for show. She's not volunteering to put anyone else down. She really is just trying to help...and sometimes that creeps me out."

She wasn't mincing words, and that made him flinch again. He'd thought this was praise, but it landed pretty harsh.

But Saki was on the money.

Sakuta felt much the same thing.

Ikumi's actions were heroic—flawlessly so.

She was the living embodiment of a "good student."

Even when she helped people, she did so unnoticed, taking no pride in it. She didn't seem to be looking for anything in return.

That was too perfect, which made it unsettling. Being that "good" was inherently creepy.

"Was she like that in junior high?"

"I didn't know her well enough to say."

"As if I do?"

Saki looked pissed.

"I'm pretty sure she was always a good student."

"And?"

"That's all I got."

"Well, that's useless."

"I know."

"Not that I expected more."

"Then don't ask."

She ignored him, glancing at her phone.

"Chiharu's begging me to come back. I'd better go."

"Suit yourself."

"You've got Ikumi covered?"

"If she needs your help again, I'm sure she'll call you herself."

That was why Saki was here at all.

"I'm asking because I know she'd never ask too much."

Saki had a good grasp on Ikumi's personality. Sometimes it creeped her out, but they were still friends, and she still worried about her. The fact that she was talking to him about it at all was likely because she'd noticed something amiss herself. This was probably part of what Yuuma found so charming about her.

He watched her go, lost in thought—then the door opened. A woman

in a white coat came out—the school doctor, who looked to be in her
midforties.

"Gotta step out," she explained before hustling off down the hall.
Had someone been hurt elsewhere? The festival was going strong, and
it would not be at all surprising if a few people got carried away
and injured themselves.

Sakuta got up and knocked on the half-open door.

"Akagi, mind if I come in?"

"Sure."

Once she answered, he went in.

It was like any hospital exam room—curtained-off beds in the
back and facilities far more professional than what could be found in
pretty much any high school. If you were brought in blindfolded, you'd
assume it was an actual hospital.

No one was there but Sakuta and Ikumi.

She was perched on the edge of a bed. The symptoms of her attack
had subsided, and she was trying to work the zipper on her back. But
with her sprained wrist, that was proving difficult.

"Need a hand?"

"……"

Her eyes stabbed through him. Guarded.

"I could call Kamisato back."

"…Don't. Please."

Saki was right. Ikumi definitely didn't want to lean on her more
than she had already.

She grabbed a fistful of hair and pulled it aside, turning her nape
toward him. The first thing he noticed was pale, clear skin. He could
see the veins running through it.

Her cheeks were slightly flushed. Her ears were turning pink. She
was trying to keep it hidden, but this was undoubtedly awkward for
her. The sooner he got it over with, the better.

"Here we go."

He grabbed the zipper and pulled it halfway down her back. This revealed the back of a white camisole, the strap fallen off one shoulder.

Her skin looked like it hadn't been exposed to the sun even once all year, but he saw marks on it like she'd been scratching an itch. The tracks ran from her right shoulder blade down her side—five lines, like fingernail marks. Left by that unseen power?

"Thanks."

She released her hair, hiding her back.

"Anything else you need?"

"If I do, I'll be calling Saki back."

With that, she grabbed the curtain and pulled it closed, driving him out.

"I have to change, so stay over there."

"Should I leave?"

"You've got questions, right?"

He heard cloth rustling beyond the curtain.

But if she was willing to let him stay, he sure didn't mind.

"That wasn't a medical condition?"

It had certainly seemed like a flare-up of something.

"The doctor says I'm healthy."

"Then what was it?"

"You already know."

Her silhouette paused.

"I can guess."

"But you want me to say it."

"I want to know what *you* think, Akagi."

"That's just mean."

She sounded defeated, yet she still didn't actually say *Adolescence Syndrome* out loud.

"It…happens every now and again."

"Honestly, I didn't really get what *was* happening."

At first, she'd seemed unwell, like she'd overexerted herself. Or was dizzy with a fever...

But what happened after that was the real problem.

"How do I put it? It's like...someone's got their hands on me."

He pictured the marks on her back. Those did look like fingernail scratches.

"Ever seen one of those shows about spooky stories as a kid? They call it a poltergeist. No one's there, but things move around."

Ikumi made that sound like a joke, but Sakuta wasn't laughing. It very much described what he'd witnessed.

Her cap flew away for no reason, then something invisible moved around beneath her clothes before finally tearing its way out from inside her stockings.

The curtains opened, and Ikumi stepped out, back in street clothes. The nurse costume was neatly folded on the bed behind her. The hole was still visible in the stockings.

"I wouldn't say it's agonizing or painful or anything like that."

Her eyes told him not to worry.

"The hand injury wasn't caused by an attack?"

Ikumi glanced down at her sprained wrist. If another attack occurred while she was trying to help someone, then it seemed all too plausible a blunder like that might happen. He could already see it playing out in his mind.

"You've got some imagination," she said, her smile uncertain.

That told him he was right.

"Leave it," she said. "I know how to fix it."

"Really?"

"Do I look like a liar?"

"You seem to have a lot of secrets."

"That, I won't deny."

Putting truth to her own words, she admitted it readily.

"You know the solution but haven't gone for it—because it's easier said than done?"

That's why her Adolescence Syndrome was still going on.

It was hard to call that okay.

"Yeah. You're not an easy man to forget."

"……"

That was unexpected. It caught him totally off guard.

"It really isn't easy," she said again, meeting his eye.

She held his gaze. It did not look like she was teasing him.

"Did you think this wasn't about you?"

"Why me?"

He didn't know why he'd be a trigger for her.

"You really don't remember."

"……"

"That was a loaded statement, I know."

Ikumi chuckled.

"We only knew each other in junior high, right?" he said.

"Mm-hmm. That's all." But her tone suggested she was neither con-firming nor denying. "There was nothing between us."

"Then why me?" he asked again.

"That is the question."

She wasn't answering. So many secrets.

"Azusagawa."

"……?"

"Fancy a wager?"

"I don't make bets I can't win."

She ignored that response entirely.

"Do I forget you first? Or do you remember what happened first?"

"What's in it for me?"

"If you remember, my Adolescence Syndrome will go away."

For the first time, she said the words.

"And you think that'll force my hand."

"Won't it?"

"Before we start this thing, let me warn you."

"What?"

"I'm pretty good at remembering things."

Twice now he'd recovered vital lost memories.

Mai.

And Shouko.

"Glad you're motivated."

"Sweeten the deal and I'll be even more motivated."

"If you win, I won't need to rely on the hashtag anymore."

"How does that work? Are you saying you save hashtag people to forget me and cure your Adolescence Syndrome?"

Ikumi nodded.

"That's why I can't quit, no matter what you say."

There was a dull gleam in her eyes. Determination, or a grim resolve. What did she make of all this? He really couldn't tell.

"If you win, what am I on the hook for?"

"Nothing at all. I'll have forgotten all about you. All you've gotta do is stay out of my life."

She smiled at him. He had no clue why that smile seemed so kind. He really had no idea what she was thinking or how she felt about all this.

"Let's get this started. Ready, set—go."

It was the least exciting starting signal he'd ever heard.

2

"I'd better get back to the flea market," Ikumi said. They left the medical office behind.

They moved silently down the hall and out the building. That hush was soon a thing of the past, as the breeze carried the noise of the crowds their way.

"Bye."

"Mm."

With that, Ikumi headed off to the flea market. Sakuta stood watching her go.

Her footsteps were sure and steady. She didn't suddenly kneel down or get attacked by a poltergeist.

When she was ten yards out, Sakuta saw someone else he knew brush past her.

Kotomi.

As they passed, Kotomi's eyes flicked to Ikumi. Like she'd spotted an old acquaintance. But she didn't stop to chat—instead, she came jogging over to Sakuta.

"Good! I found you."

Apparently, she'd been looking for him. It had been over an hour since he left Mai's side. Mai, Kaede, and Kotomi must have split up to scour the campus. There was sweat on Kotomi's brow that somehow seemed out of place with the crisp fall breeze blowing.

"Sorry to drag you into this."

"No prob," she said firmly.

Then she stole a hesitant glance over her shoulder. Ikumi had already disappeared down the row of stalls.

"That was…Ikumi, right?" she asked.

Naming the girl she'd just seen him with.

"You knew her, Kano?"

There'd been a two-year age gap, but Kotomi had been at their junior high, so it wasn't all that strange.

"Same high school."

Kotomi had moved on to a local public prep school. The boys wore your standard black *gakuran*, but the girls wore a gray blazer not often seen in those parts; anyone who lived nearby knew exactly which school they went to.

"We helped prep the sports festival together. We didn't spend all that much time together, but…"

Kotomi stared after Ikumi, a sad look in her eyes. Perhaps she was disappointed that Ikumi hadn't recognized her.

"I doubt she expected to see you here."

If someone wasn't on your radar, they were easy to overlook. Same principle that kept Mai from getting spotted all the time in public.

"…The two of you were close?" Kotomi asked, glancing back at him—a bit rattled. Anyone who knew Kaede's bullying history would probably have the same look.

They would assume Sakuta didn't want to dwell on memories of junior high.

And that wasn't exactly wrong. If anything, it was right on the money.

"We barely spoke at the time. No hostility or anything, but…now it's more like, 'Oh right, we were in the same junior high!'"

It was hard to be any more precise than that. His own position was fairly vague, and he was even less sure where Ikumi stood. They'd gone to the same junior high and wound up at the same college. And for now, he had no words to define things beyond that basic truth.

But now that they had this weird wager going, it was apparent something lay between them that Sakuta had forgotten. And what Kotomi knew about Ikumi might help him remember.

"What was Akagi like in high school?"

"That's a broad question. Uh, first I'd better tell Kae I found you."

Kotomi took out her phone and quickly typed out a message. "Where are we?" she asked.

"Outside the first building," Sakuta said.

Kotomi and Kaede exchanged a couple texts, and then Kotomi closed the cover on her phone.

"You wanna know about Ikumi?"

"Yeah."

"When I started in spring, she was the student president. She made a speech to the new students, and I remember thinking third-years seemed so grown-up."

This news did not come as a surprise. Ikumi was totally the type to run for that office. And he could easily see her giving a speech before a sea of new students without batting an eye.

"But in hindsight, that had less to do with being a third-year and more Ikumi just being Ikumi."

"Yeah."

Looking back from college really put into perspective that they were definitely still just kids back in high school.

"Ikumi was real big on area volunteer work."

"So she was always like that?"

"Mm?"

"She's founded another volunteer group here, helping tutor kids who won't go to school."

"Sounds like her. She's the kind of person who steps up and does the thing the rest of us just wait for someone else to handle. Everyone in her year relied on her, said she was amazing."

"Amazing, hmm?"

Kotomi hadn't used the word out of pure enthusiasm. There was a trace of something else behind it. Definitely a hint of "That's one way to describe it."

"But Akagi made the most of her time in high school, then," he said.

She'd been class president, and if she'd helped out with the sports festival, she'd likely been involved with all the big-deal events.

And the fact that she was at this university proved she'd done pretty well for herself academically. Her being in the nursing school implied this had been her first choice.

That was what he meant, but Kotomi looked a little uncomfortable with the phrase.

"Am I wrong?"

"Not exactly, but…"

"But?"

"About this time last year, she got summoned by the school counselor. Several times."

That didn't sound like her at all.

The counselor?

Ikumi Akagi seemed like the kind of person who'd never even set foot in that office.

"Do you know why?"

"Well, I know what the rumors were."

"I'll take it with a grain of salt, then."

"Supposedly, she had an older boyfriend and was living with him, never going home at all."

"If that's true, she was making the most of life in *and* out of school."

"You…think so?"

Kotomi was clearly less sure.

"I mean, she was school president, the center of her class, helping people with volunteer work, passing her entrance exams, madly in love, and getting chewed out by teachers. That's like student life bingo, right there."

A résumé like that could give any coming-of-age film a run for its money.

Sadly, the boyfriend part felt like a total fabrication. He based that on how she'd acted in the medical office. If she'd lived with a man for a while, getting help with a zipper wouldn't have flustered her nearly as much.

More likely she had her reasons for not going home and was crashing with a female friend instead. Nothing crazier than that. That made more sense to him.

"Oh, there's Kae!"

Kotomi waved, and he spotted Kaede and Mai coming down the ginkgoes.

"Thanks, Komi! Sakuta, where'd you wander off to?"

Kaede had her cheeks puffed up like he was the troublemaker here.

"I didn't wander."

He'd had his reasons, but he hadn't told her any of them, so her attitude was justified.

She grumbled a bit longer but wanted to see more of the festival. She and Kotomi soon went off together.

Leaving Mai and Sakuta alone together.

"Glad Kaede's enjoying herself."

"She's a Zukki stan, so I was all worried she'd try to apply here."

Kaede was in her second year of high school. It was about time she started narrowing down her options.

"Well, you can help tutor her."

"That's what I'm worried about."

He was doing that for money, but at the moment, his students were all first-years. Frankly, he was hoping to avoid teaching any exam students. The responsibility was grave.

"That aside...you found Akagi?"

She gave him a searching look and put the straw of her bubble tea to her lips.

"I did."

"Well?"

Chewing the tapioca, she held the cup out his way. He took a sip and got a mouthful of pearls. Pushing them around his mouth, he admitted, "I get her even less now."

"Oh dear," Mai said before inhaling more tapioca.

"My feelings exactly."

The texture of the tapioca really ruined any tension this conversation might have had.

3

When Sakuta woke up the next morning, the sun was already high in the sky.

It was 11:50.

First period had come and gone, and second period was about to end. If he hustled out of here, he might make it in time for third.

But instead of panicking, he yawned and closed his eyes.

What with all the festival cleanup, there were no classes today. It was like having a holiday.

He enjoyed lying around for a while longer, then got up.

He found a note from Kaede on the dining room table saying she was at work. Taking shifts on a weekday morning was the kind of trick remote learning enabled. She could pick when to study and when to work of her own free will. And Kaede was taking full advantage of it.

Sakuta soloed a lunch that looked like breakfast, vacuumed with a noon news program blaring, then hung the laundry on the veranda.

The dry fall air would make short work of these clothes.

When he took them in later, it was almost five.

"She should be home soon."

He picked up the receiver and punched eleven digits in by heart.

It rang three times.

"What?" Rio growled, less than enthusiastic.

"Where are you now?"

"Just back in Fujisawa."

"Got time before your lesson?"

Her class started at seven.

"I'll be busy browsing the bookstore."

"Then wait there. I'll join you."

"I'll leave the moment I'm done."

Sakuta hung up, pretending he hadn't heard that last bit.

In the electronics store by Fujisawa Station's north exit, he took escalators up to the seventh floor—which offered a different view.

Bookshelves ran in every direction, and that quiet library hush hung in the air. This was probably the largest bookstore in the area, and Rio came here often.

He'd figured this was what she meant, but there was no sign of her in the section packed with physics tomes.

"Did she really leave already?"

Worried, he did a quick scan of the rest of the store. He found Rio standing by the college exam study guides.

"Sitting exams again?" he said, parking himself next to her.

"My student is."

She snapped the book closed and returned it to the shelf. Apparently, it hadn't met her exacting standards.

"And this student would be…?"

"Kunimi's kohai, the one you asked about."

"Toranosuke Kasai."

"Wow, you actually remembered."

"It's hard to forget."

"……"

Rio's look suggested she'd caught him hiding something, but she didn't bother digging. Must have decided it was something dumb.

"You ask how he decided on his school of choice?"

"He said it just felt right."

"Ha."

"So what do you want?"

He'd rather have talked about Toranosuke a bit longer, but if he tried anything, she might catch on. Clueing her in would just ruin all the boy's clumsy attempts to hide it.

So he moved on to his actual goal here.

"So…"

"Are you sure it wasn't the invisible man?" Rio said after he explained the baffling stuff that happened to Ikumi yesterday. "I mean, it's not like you haven't already met someone invisible."

She meant the miniskirt Santa. Who was still being actively invisible.

"Touko Kirishima wasn't with us."

Or at least, he'd been unable to see her. No one but the two of them had been in arm's length. But something had definitely been in contact with Ikumi.

"What did she say?"

"Made jokes about poltergeists."

"So she was taking it in stride."

"Weird body stuff is closest to Kaede's case, I guess?"

Her classmates' heartless words had been like knives cutting Kaede's skin, and the pain in her own heart caused gnarly bruises to appear all over her.

"But this left no marks on her?"

"There were scratches on her back, running from her shoulder blade to her side."

"…You saw that?"

Rio's voice dropped to a growl.

"I was helping her change."

"……"

"I just lowered the zipper on her back!"

"Did you tell Sakurajima that?"

"Can we keep it between us?"

"……"

That silence seemed ominous.

"But at the very least, it didn't seem to be causing Akagi any pain. She herself said it wasn't painful or agonizing."

He didn't think she was lying. Even if this had similarities to Kaede's case, the core Adolescence Syndrome symptoms might be fundamentally different.

"From this, I can't say much of anything. It's all too vague."

"If you've got nothing, I'm up shit creek."

"Sounds like you don't really get her yourself, Azusagawa."

"Yeah…"

That was the real reason he was feeling lost here. Sakuta just didn't have a good handle on who Ikumi Akagi was. There was no way for him to dive deeper into her Adolescence Syndrome, either. What emotions were giving rise to this supernatural stuff? That remained a mystery.

"But if what she said was true, I know one thing for sure."

"That's my Futaba! What?"

Rio just gave him a look.

"I thought you would've noticed," she said.

"What?"

"She was in love with you. Bad enough she'd want to forget that."

"…But there was nothing between us."

Not that he'd been aware of.

"There are girls out there who get shot down with a single chocolate cornet."

"…Can't argue with experience."

If it had been something simple like that, it stood to reason he couldn't remember.

But he didn't think he belonged in the same category as Yuuma with his dreamboat hunkiness.

"Better get those memories back before her ghost comes after you."

Having seen the poltergeist in action, he didn't find her comment remotely funny.

Leaving Rio to peruse the other guides, Sakuta headed down the escalators. He went out the doors on the second floor of the electronics shop below and stepped onto the elevated walkway to the station.

There was a flood of foot traffic as students and workers on their way home streamed out the north exit.

Fighting against the tide, Sakuta went down the stairs on the side that led away from his home. He had a shift at the restaurant next.

Walking down the commercial district past cram schools, drug stores, and cafés, he saw the yellow sign of his workplace up ahead.

And someone he knew was coming out.

She saw Sakuta approaching and stopped outside the restaurant. She was a woman in her forties and had maybe put on a few pounds. More specifically, it was Miwako Tomobe, a school counselor who'd helped Kaede a lot.

"Sakuta, long time no see. You're looking all grown up."

"Am I?"

He saw himself too often to really notice. But it had been a solid six months since they'd seen each other, so maybe he did look different.

"You stopped by to check on Kaede?"

She'd kept in touch even after Kaede graduated, and when she heard she was waiting tables, she'd popped by the restaurant a few times.

"I was in the area."

"Well, thanks."

"Visiting Kaede really picks me up. Working all on her own, really enjoying it—it's nice to see."

"You helped a lot."

"She worked hard. And you were really there for her!"

"Let's say it was all of that."

Trading compliments always made him fidget.

"How's college?"

"I'm getting by."

"Good to hear."

She looked relieved. But that soon passed. She glanced at him, and her lips moved as if silently saying "Oh," like seeing him had jogged her memory. But she didn't say anything. There was a hint of hesitation in her eyes.

"What?"

He wasn't sure what she might have to say after all this time. So he waited for her.

"Do you happen to know Ikumi Akagi?" she asked, her tone much more serious.

"……Mm?"

He blinked at her. That was the last name he'd expected to hear. Had Miwako really brought her up? That shocked him so much he refused to believe it.

"How do you know her, Ms. Tomobe?"

"Last month, I started helping with the volunteer group she founded. Not with the tutoring, but with the mental health side."

"Ah, that explains it."

The pin fell into place. Ikumi was working with kids who'd stopped going to school. Having an actual school counselor involved would really help.

"When we first met, she mentioned where she'd gone to junior high."

"And that tied her to me?"

"Yeah." Miwako nodded, her eyes on Sakuta. She seemed worried about him.

She had a pretty good idea what Kaede's troubles had led to and how Sakuta had been treated by his own classmates.

And she knew he wouldn't welcome being reunited with any of them. A logical conclusion.

"Anything bothering you?"

"Nope."

There was. Ikumi was using the dreaming hashtag to play hero and getting attacked by an Adolescence Syndrome poltergeist.

But that wasn't what Miwako was asking about. She was asking about *him*. If the encounter had resurfaced any old traumas.

"Did Akagi strike you as the kind of person who'd talk shit about me?"

"No."

She was quite clear on that.

"I haven't known her long, but she's the serious, righteous type."

"I agree."

They certainly had similar impressions of her. Saki had said much the same thing; likely everyone Ikumi Akagi had ever met did.

"That might lead to her hurting people sometimes…but she's pretty aware of how people react."

"Yeah."

Raising the flag of righteousness meant clashing with people who insist you're forcing your values down their throats. But he was pretty sure Ikumi would manage to avoid that kind of conflict. Like Miwako implied, she knew what to watch out for.

"But doesn't that get exhausting?" he asked.

"Having everyone think you're serious and righteous?"

"She knows exactly what everyone thinks of her."

Like Miwako said, she was "aware."

Ikumi would know what those looks meant.

Perhaps she'd even tried to adjust herself to them.

Trying to live up to expectations could weigh on a person. Like how Nodoka had suffered in high school, when her mother constantly compared her with Mai.

Could that be the cause of her Adolescence Syndrome?

"Akagi was born serious, so people around her started describing her accordingly. Or did they tell her she was serious, so she started acting the way they wanted? Hard to say which came first. But in Akagi's case, she's living up to those expectations, and it seems like she finds that fulfilling."

Sure, if everyone relies on you and comes to you for help and you can live up to all of that—then you might very well end each day feeling like you've accomplished something. And that helps keep you going, letting you face the next day with your head held high. Letting you stay serious and righteous.

But still, Ikumi clearly had *something* causing her severe mental stress. Enough to manifest this Adolescence Syndrome poltergeist.

"If Akagi did have problems, what do you imagine they'd be?"

"Why do you ask?"

Miwako raised an eyebrow at him.

"Her friends said she's been acting a bit off lately."

He couldn't exactly say the truth, so he went with a brazen lie, picturing Saki's grumpy face.

"I guess the first thing that comes to mind…would be romantic problems."

Her lips curled up in a smile. But Rio had already worked that angle. He didn't need more.

"Anything else?" he asked.

"Well…" Miwako broke off, then looked at him, hesitating.

"I'm involved?"

"She might not have wanted to run into you."

"……"

"I could see her inability to help you being the great failure of her life."

"I didn't go to her for help."

He had begged his class to believe the Adolescence Syndrome affecting Kaede. But he'd never gone to Ikumi personally. Never directly addressed any individual girl.

Yet part of him thought Miwako's words made perfect sense.

Ikumi *would* feel responsible.

She couldn't stand seeing other people hurting.

And that was why she wanted to forget him.

That likely didn't mean she literally wanted him excised from her memories. That wasn't physically possible anyway. The more you want to forget something, the more it gets seared into your brain. That's how human minds work.

When Ikumi said *forget*, she meant overcoming past regrets, turning them into a thing of the past.

Putting her third year of junior high behind her.

Now that she had Adolescence Syndrome of her own, she knew everything Sakuta had said was true. She was all too aware of what she'd done wrong. But she couldn't fix that now.

The entire class had turned on Sakuta. They had rejected him. He'd lost count of how many times people had called him crazy.

Now? Ikumi knew they'd been wrong. But where did that leave her?

Was she beating herself up over past failures? Enough to wish she could forget him?

"You've got a shift, Sakuta? I'm not keeping you, am I?"

Miwako checked the time.

"I'm running early. Plenty of time."

"Well, good."

"Um, Ms. Tomobe…"

"Mm?"

"I got a favor to ask."

"What?"

"Next time you go to this volunteer group, can you bring me along?"

Thinking wasn't getting him anywhere so he decided to ask the girl herself.

4

"Bye, Ikumi-sensei!"

"Take care."

Ikumi was out in the hall, waving good-bye to the junior high kids. Two boys and a girl, the same ones who'd been at the campus festival flea market. Ikumi's right arm was no longer in a sling. Like she'd said, it had only taken a week to heal.

Once her students were out of sight, she let out a dramatic sigh. That was for Sakuta's benefit.

He didn't have to ask if she'd done that on purpose.

It was the weekend after he'd bumped into Miwako outside the restaurant—Saturday, November 12.

Sakuta and Ikumi were both on their college campus at Kanazawa-hakkei. Specifically, he had come through the main gates, turned right, and headed toward the glass building in the back. It had been built quite recently with an eye on local outreach. Most people simply called it Hall 8.

He'd heard it was used for volunteer groups or off-campus clubs, but this was his first time seeing the building in person.

"Sorry for not warning you about him," Miwako said as Ikumi came back in. He'd talked her into just saying someone wanted to observe her volunteer work, without mentioning Sakuta's name.

"No, this isn't on you, Ms. Tomobe."

Evidently, she blamed *him*. He pretended not to notice. If he didn't notice, the implication was lost to the world.

"Oh? Then can I leave this to the two of you?"

She glanced at both of them and then shouldered her purse, saying she had places to be.

"Go on. Thanks for coming."

"See you next week."

Miwako left, fluttering her half-raised hand. They listened to her footsteps retreat into the distance until they were no longer audible.

That left Sakuta and Ikumi alone with the silence.

"……"

"……"

Without a word, Ikumi began erasing formulas from the white-board. They had been working on a basic factorization problem.

Sakuta stepped forward and started to help.

"Akagi, you mad at me?"

It didn't show, but that sigh had definitely been reproachful.

"We've got that wager going," she said, in a regular tone of voice.

"Yeah."

"And what were the terms of it?"

"Seeing if you can forget me before I remember you."

"And if you keep wandering around in front of me, I can't forget you no matter how hard I try."

"A gambler's life is hard."

"I didn't take you for the competitive type."

That line was a bit more forceful. She finished erasing the board, having not looked his way once. What an awkward way to fume.

"I said I don't take bets I can't win."

"You did *not* mean it at the time."

She gathered up the black, red, and blue dry-erase markers and put them away in a case. Then she absently glanced at the clock—and her eyes widened, as if what she'd seen was bad news.

Sakuta followed her gaze.

It was 3:40 PM.

When he looked back down, she finally met his eyes.

"You got somewhere to be?" he asked.

"You sure have a sharp eye."

"The life of a hero sure is a busy one."

"Will you stop that?"

"You're still going, right?"

"Yeah," she agreed, attempting a smile.

"The lost little girl in Yokosuka? Or the railroad crossing accident? There was a stolen bicycle, too."

"……You've done your homework."

Her smile stiffened.

"Were you gonna hit all three?"

The three dream tweets he'd found had times far enough apart that if she headed out now, she could probably make it.

"I've really gotta run," she said, clearly done answering questions. She was already headed to the door.

He called after her anyway.

"How many you gotta rescue before your regret disappears?"

"……"

She froze in the doorway.

"…Did you remember something?" she asked, not turning back.

"I just figured not helping me in junior high's the sort of thing *you'd* still be dragging around."

Miwako had put the idea in his head, and it wasn't really based on anything tangible. But the words got her to turn and face him.

"I…!"

She spun around, gaze locked on his. Her emotions stabbed into him. But her eyes wavered anxiously, and she looked ready to cry.

He didn't know what she was going through. The only thing he was certain of was that in this moment, she was more emotional than he'd ever seen her be.

But the glimpse beneath her calm mask was soon painted over by a different emotion.

Before any further words emerged from her lips, a shiver ran down her spine—and she clapped both hands over her mouth as she crouched down.

"Akagi…? Is this…"

He remembered what happened at the festival.

The poltergeist.

Sakuta ran over to her, and the hair hanging down her back went from straight to gathered. Then it turned, twisting, the ends pointed upward like she was submerged in a bath.

Neither Sakuta nor Ikumi was touching her hair. And it was held firmly together without a single hairpin.

"Again…not now…!"

She moved her hand from her mouth to her thigh and pinched it hard. It was painful to watch. Who was she talking to?

Then he saw a snakelike something moving beneath her blouse. It traveled down her throat, across her shoulders, and into her sleeve. There was no one here, but the folds of her clothes writhed and let him track it.

The door and windows were open, but there was no breeze. Neither of them was touching her sleeve. There was nothing there, yet it was moving like ripples on the water.

"……"

Seeing the poltergeist firsthand again had his heart in turmoil, and he didn't know what to say to her.

He couldn't move. His mind was held captive by the strange phenomenon in front of him. He was beyond shock. His blood simply ran cold. Unadulterated fear of the unknown raged through his head. It was just that unsettling.

Yet his hand reached out on its own.

Trying to grab the invisible snake, it got a firm grip on the twisting wrist of her left hand.

"?!"

But all he felt was Ikumi's surprise and the thinness of her wrist.

"Sorry, Akagi," he said, and before she could respond, he rolled up her sleeve to her elbow.

Nothing there. The snake didn't exist.

"......?!"

But what he *did* see there raised another wave of questions and surprises.

For some reason, her pale skin was covered in letters, like they'd been written with Magic Marker.

——*You okay there?*

——*Sorry 'bout the sprain.*

——*Watch yourself with him.*

——*It's all going well.*

They almost seemed like texts.

"Is this...?"

He looked to her for an answer.

"Let go...!" she whispered.

Sakuta still had a firm grip on her wrist.

He released it.

Then the letters on her arm began running, like she was under a shower, moving from her elbow to her wrist and vanishing.

Ikumi pulled her sleeve down, hiding the red mark on her wrist where he'd held her.

"Was that part of the poltergeist?"

That was definitely not reminders like some kid might write on their hands to remember what they needed for school tomorrow.

"Nothing good comes of spending time with you, Azusagawa."

"So I really am the cause."

The previous poltergeist incident had also happened while he was watching. Because he'd sent ripples through her heart. Because he'd caused her stress. The math worked out.

"Like I said, I know how to fix it."

She was obviously pushing him away.

"So you know what this poltergeist is?"

"……"

She didn't answer, but silence *was* the answer.

"That's why you're sure you're fine."

Something this outlandish would normally drive you around the bend.

Ikumi was able to handle it *because* she knew exactly what it was. And that it wasn't something that would do her harm. And if it was using words, it was *human*.

Which left one question.

"Who is it?"

"……"

Ikumi didn't answer.

He felt like he was getting closer to the truth.

"If I tell you, it'll affect the wager."

She said that but the way Sakuta saw it, he hadn't made any progress at all.

Sakuta still had no clue who Ikumi really was. What was going through her mind, how she felt about all this—Ikumi Akagi herself remained an enigma.

No matter what angle he came at her from, the impenetrable walls she had up prevented him from getting any closer.

He was just walking in circles around those walls, gazing up at the castle she lived in. Not even sure she actually lived in it.

Ultimately, he was forced to retreat again, with nothing to show for it. Feeling like there was nothing he could do without someone rolling in with reinforcements.

No end in sight.

Perhaps that was the whole reason Ikumi had set this wager in the first place.

But as he thought that—

"Ikumi."

—someone called her name.

Sakuta looked up and saw a man standing in the hall. Early twenties. He was wearing a suit, so he'd probably already entered the workforce. About Sakuta's height, bespectacled. Diligent looking.

"I said we were done seeing each other," Ikumi said, straightening up. The poltergeist subsided.

"Sorry. I just…had to talk."

"I'm afraid I've got places to be."

She picked her bag off the floor and slipped past the man without so much as making eye contact.

He started to reach for her but seemed to think better of it.

Ikumi's footsteps soon vanished down the stairs.

It was plain to see these two had history.

If this man knew Ikumi, talking to him might help. But how to start that conversation?

While Sakuta dithered, the man's gaze settled on him.

"Are you…Azusagawa?"

"……"

He had not expected a total stranger—especially one not even a student here—to know his name.

But he was grateful for the opener.

"And you are…?"

"I used to date her," the man admitted, eyes turned the way she'd gone.

"So you're…"

"Her ex."

The man looked uncomfortable, then tried to cover that with a smile.

Five minutes later, Sakuta was on a bench outside.

On the gingko lane.

The soccer team was practicing on the field opposite. The coach yelled, "Footwork!"

It was Saturday, but there were still quite a few students on campus strolling up and down the lane. The two men going past must have been science seniors. "I can't get this thesis done!" "I'm *just* as doomed."

"Ah, the thesis. That was a nightmare."

The voice came from Sakuta's side.

The other man was sitting on the bench, a distinct space between them.

The man who called himself Ikumi's ex.

He'd said he was waiting for someone and followed Sakuta out.

His name was Seiichi Takasaka. He'd introduced himself on the way here.

His business card bore the name of a company Sakuta had never heard of and an equally obscure division within.

Sakuta glanced sideways and found Seiichi with an unlit cigarette in his lips.

"Mind if I smoke?" he asked, catching the glance. He was already reaching for the lighter in his pocket.

"Can I ask you not to?"

"Mm?"

"This is a nonsmoking area."

That was a whole new thing here in college. The campus had clear divisions between areas where you could smoke and areas you couldn't. The smoking areas were by the club building, behind the science building, and over by the labs.

Most students turned twenty during their time here. That meant they could legally smoke. Quite a few students darted out for a puff during their breaks.

"Oh really?"

Seiichi put the cigarette back in the box, wincing. He'd been making some variation on this expression the whole time. It was probably an expression of his discomfort at having a witness to his attempt to talk to Ikumi.

"I don't usually smoke. But when I'm tense or need a distraction…"

As he made excuses, he put the yellow box back in his suit pocket. Seiichi didn't smell like smoke, so this was likely true.

"So when I do smoke, I wind up coughing, and everyone's just like, 'Stop, then!'"

Seiichi kept talking without Sakuta asking a thing. It wasn't really for Sakuta's benefit, and it didn't seem like he cared much if Sakuta was listening. It was like the cigarettes. Just a tic to hide his discomfort.

"When did you and Akagi meet?"

"When she was volunteering in her first year of high school. I asked her out in her second."

"She mentioned me?"

"I forget why. She showed me her junior high graduation album once. It was kind of like a guessing game, seeing if I could figure out who she'd been friends with and who her first crush was."

"And you were unlucky enough to point at me?"

"Yep. And her smile faded fast."

"That sure makes it sound like there was *something*."

But to Sakuta's knowledge, they'd barely had any contact. Not been in love, not had any big fights nor any bittersweet memories of youth.

Kaede had been bullied and developed Adolescence Syndrome, and nobody in class had believed the truth, leaving Sakuta ostracized.

"She told me a bit about what went down in her third-year class. Seemed like she was still hung up on you a bit, so it stuck with me. Maybe I was just jealous."

Seiichi turned toward him as he spoke, which made Sakuta look back.

"Didn't ever think I'd meet you myself."

"I didn't expect to meet Akagi's ex, either."

Kotomi had told him about the boyfriend thing, but forget half believing it—he hadn't even managed 20 percent. And was genuinely shocked to find it was true.

"What's your relationship with her, Azusagawa? Uh, are you seeing each other?"

"Nothing like that, no."

"Oh…"

Seiichi's eyes dropped to the ground. He looked a little relieved, but also a little forlorn. How had he taken that answer? Sakuta wasn't sure.

But there was one thing that came across loud and clear: Seiichi still loved her.

"Why'd you split up?"

"Short answer—my fault."

"Is the long answer any different?"

"Well, I'm still the bad guy," Seiichi said with a chuckle. At least half of that was him laughing at himself. "The day she graduated high school, she told me we were done seeing each other. On this thing, out of the blue."

He pulled his phone out of his pocket.

"And you just accepted that?"

"I figured I didn't have any right to argue."

"Why is that?"

"Last year, I was a senior and really struggling to land a job. Didn't have time for her."

"The job search is that rough?"

Last term, he'd seen a lot of seniors in suits on campus. Post-festival, there were almost none left.

"It was for me. It's a seller's market, so the smart ones landed a tentative offer at a big company and goofed off."

It sounded like he was talking about a specific friend. He had a very sour expression on his face.

"I did employment exams at fifty places and failed them all. By the fifty-first place, I was all out of things to say. I mean, what the hell is your fifty-first choice?"

"Yeah."

"They ask why'd you apply to us, and it's not like you've got a reason. I started with the big names you've heard of and compromised when that didn't work, and kept moving down the list when *that* didn't. Rinse and repeat fifty times and I stopped caring. Just give me a damn job, I thought. And the interviewers could tell that's where I was at. They knew I was still left on the shelf in November, December."

"……"

Having never been involved in that kind of hiring season, Sakuta didn't know what to say. He just waited for more.

"I had some confidence before I went in. After starting college, I did volunteer work and thought I knew more about the world than most students. But after being told I wasn't wanted fifty times, I didn't even know how to promote myself. And everyone I knew was landing tentative offers, so I was starting to panic…"

Seiichi's voice was getting gloomier and gloomier. He'd started his story as if it were a funny anecdote about past trials, but…

"And while that was happening, you and Akagi…?" Sakuta asked, getting it back on track.

"She was there for me the whole time. She'd come over, cook, iron my interview shirts. Wake me up when I had an early call before the alarm even rang, made lunches for me."

"……"

Honestly, this part came as a bit of a surprise. He still hadn't been convinced *all* of Kotomi's story was true.

"And she never once wished me luck on my way out to an interview."

She must have thought that would add to the pressure.

A very Ikumi thing to do.

"When I got back, she'd just say, 'Welcome home.' Not 'How'd it go?' She never let it show, either. Even though her entrance exams must have left her just as strung out."

He could totally see Ikumi doing that. Supporting her boyfriend but never slacking off on her own studying. Her clear moral compass included herself, which meant she was never allowed to cut corners. She'd likely never even considered taking time off.

"I still don't know what ultimately did you in."

So far, he'd just been bragging about his ex.

"The more stressed out I got, the more I started to resent her."

"……"

"I remember Christmas Eve. I saw her studying in her room and felt like that was silent criticism of me. Before I knew it, I'd told her not to come by for a while."

"That's pretty bad."

"I entirely agree."

But everyone had the blood rush to their head sometimes. If you blew the first move, what mattered most was the second. A second blunder could be fatal.

"I should have apologized right away. But I wasn't mature enough to do that. I believed I couldn't afford to do anything else that would make me look weak, but that was just me being weak."

"Yeah." Sakuta nodded.

Seiichi let out a wheezy laugh there. Acknowledging that Sakuta's blunt agreement felt better than any attempts to play nice.

"But you did get hired," Sakuta said, gaze dropping to the card in his hands. That proved it.

"After the New Year, finally."

"You told her?"

"I figured I should leave her be until exams were over. And the upshot..."

"While you were waiting, she broke up with you?"

National universities often announced their exam results in mid-March. High school graduation ceremonies came first. Sakuta's had.

"That she did." Seiichi nodded. The biggest wince of the day. A bitter look at his own past failures.

"So why come see her now?"

It made sense that it had taken time to sort through things, but if there was another reason, he'd like to know. That might give Sakuta a clue to his forgotten past with Ikumi.

"I saw her tweets."

"......"

"That sounded creepy, huh?"

"A bit."

"That's how the world sees it. That's why I didn't want to say anything...but it said she had a dream where she got someone hurt and was arrested for it."

"Akagi, arrested?"

Both hurting people and trouble with the police did not sound like Ikumi at all. He had to ask.

"You've heard stories about the dreaming hashtag?"

"You believe that stuff?"

"Not really something grown-ups believe, is it? But I couldn't get it out of my mind."

Sakuta understood that. What if it *did* come true? And since Sakuta had experience with something like prophetic dreams, he really couldn't dismiss these things.

"Do you know the date?"

"Hang on."

Seiichi pulled out of his phone and hunted for the tweet in question.

"November twenty-seventh."

That date rang a bell.

Ikumi had passed along the invite to a class reunion held that day.

A junior high reunion.

With *that* class...

Coincidence? Or...

"Since I saw that tweet, I got all nervous. Felt like I shouldn't have left her on her own."

His lingering feelings for her were evident in his tone.

"Being there for others is what keeps her going."

He said that mostly to himself, but the idea wormed its way into Sakuta's thoughts, permeating his being.

"Maybe, yeah."

Agreement came after the fact.

Helping other people was how she helped herself. That matched his concept of Ikumi.

That was why her heroic actions had always felt so risky.

That was why she couldn't stop.

If she ever stopped helping, she'd collapse.

"Takasaka…"

"Mm?"

"Do you still care about Akagi?"

"I know I *should* have let her go by now…" Seiichi got to his feet. He was checking the time on his phone—maybe he was supposed to be at work. "Right, if it's not too much to ask, can I get your contact info? Let me know if anything happens with her. If it gets to be a problem, feel free to block me."

His fingers were running across the screen, likely firing up a chat app.

"Sorry, I don't have a phone."

"Huh?"

This fact always came as a surprise to people.

"That's not an awkward way of saying no. I just got sick of it all in junior high and haven't carried one since."

The original motivation for this decision was long since gone. But since he was getting by fine without one, he'd never been motivated to pick one up.

"Oh."

Seiichi looked momentarily at a loss but soon gave up and pocketed his phone.

"Then if the stars align."

"Yep."

Both of them probably assumed they would never meet again. Seiichi headed off toward the front gate. He neither paused nor looked back. Why would he? There was nothing to be gained from that.

Sakuta didn't bother watching him for long. But he had a good reason not to. He sensed someone sitting next to him, and his mind turned that way.

Not just any old someone. A *red* someone.

A miniskirt Santa was occupying the seat Seiichi had vacated. Her legs were crossed, an arm propped on them, chin in hand. She was looking at him through long lashes.

"It's Saturday. What are you doing on campus?"

"Being surprised by the sudden manifestation of a miniskirt Santa."

"Ew."

Touko rolled her eyes at him. He'd meant it, so this seemed unwarranted. But running into her suited his purposes. He had loads of question for Touko Kirishima.

"What did you do to Akagi?"

"I merely gave her a present. Everyone wants presents."

"Santa Claus handles poltergeist distribution?"

"Hardly," Touko laughed. "That is *not* her Adolescence Syndrome."

Sakuta had been starting to think that himself. The letters written on her arm bore signs of a personality, of someone else's will. Pretty different from your standard hauntings. Those words were a clear attempt at communication.

"Well, what is it?"

"Santa's not allowed to blab people's secrets."

Touko held his gaze, her smile a challenge.

"Is the dreaming hashtag also your fault?"

If she wouldn't talk about Ikumi, he'd just have to try another approach.

"Everyone worries about the future."

"So you show them dreams about it?"

"Don't make me repeat myself. I'm not showing anything. They're doing that on their own."

This was getting him nowhere. He'd finally met her again but was learning nada.

"No more questions?" she asked, yawning. There was a phone in her hand now. She was working it one-handed. Santa Claus was a smartphone pro.

"Then one more."

"What?"

She didn't look up from the screen.

"Give me your phone number."

"……"

Her thumb froze midswipe.

Then she gave him some side-eye.

"Oh, should I tell you mine first?"

"No thanks."

Flatly rejecting his offer, Touko shifted her focus back to her phone. This was a nonstarter. Her attitude made that clear.

"What was your major again?" she asked abruptly.

"Statistical science."

"Is that a math thing?"

She didn't even look up.

"It could be described that way."

"If you're an egghead, then do you have pi memorized?"

"I know 3.1415926535 at least."

"Good enough."

He was unclear what convinced her, but she thrust her screen in his face, saying, "Three, two…"

A very short countdown.

There were eleven digits on her screen. A number starting with 090.

"One, zero! Time's up!"

She yanked her wrist back, hiding the screen.

"One more time."

"That was your only chance! Also, we're being interrupted."

Touko turned to the footsteps coming up from behind.

"Hey," Mai said, stepping into view.

"How was your remedial class, Mai?"

"That is not what this was! The professor rescheduled a class that got canceled earlier this term!"

She reached out and twisted his cheek.

"Of course, I was filming on the original date, so this works in my favor."

Mai let go of him and looked at the seat next to him.

"Were you talking to someone?"

"See for yourself. Touko Kirishima——"

He found himself gesturing to an empty seat.

"……"

He did a 360 scan of his surroundings and found no miniskirt Santas. She'd vanished into thin air.

"She was here?" Mai asked, also looking around.

"Yep, definitely."

"Huh…"

Sure felt like a trickster spirit at work. He'd had more questions for her…but no use getting dejected now. He *had* remembered all eleven digits.

"What happened with Akagi?"

"A lot. Also met her ex-boyfriend."

"Her what?"

"It's a long story."

He got to his feet.

"Then tell me on the way home."

"Oh, about that."

"Mm?"

"I was thinking about stopping by my parents' place."

He'd gotten rid of everything from junior high, graduation album included. There was nothing to find by going home. It wasn't even the same place they'd lived at the time.

But it had been a small neighborhood. It's possible his parents remembered something about Ikumi.

Parents had their own social networks.

And that thing about her getting arrested was hard to ignore.

"Then let's get some beaker pudding from Yokohama Station."

"Mm? Mai, you're coming?"

"I haven't been by since that time last summer. Come on."

Mai headed off without seeing what he thought.

And that meant he had no choice but to fall in line.

5

Sakuta rang the intercom on his parents' place. There was a five-second delay, and then his father answered.

"It's me," Sakuta said, putting his face near the little lens.

"Oh. Be right there."

The interphone cut out, and he heard footsteps coming. The lock turned, and the door swung open.

There stood his father, a sandal on one foot. It was Saturday, but he was still in slacks and a collared shirt.

"What brings you here?"

"A son can't come home without a reason?"

Sakuta was the family's kid.

"Of course you can, but…"

"Hello," Mai said, stepping into view before he could say more. "Nice to be here."

"Oh, hi. Hello, Mai. You came, too?"

She hadn't been on the interphone's camera, and his father was clearly rattled.

"Sakuta, you should warn…," he began, but then he caught Mai's look and let it drop. Not an argument to have in front of your son's girlfriend. "Come on in."

He held the door open, waving them both through.

"Dear, it's Sakuta and Mai!" he called.

The apartment had a standard two-bedroom layout.

"Really? How nice to see you!"

Sakuta's mother was sitting at the dining table just inside the entrance.

"Sorry to drop by unannounced," Mai said, bowing her head.

"Don't worry about it. Welcome home, Sakuta."

"Nice to be back. We brought presents."

They'd bought pudding in the Yokohama Station department store basement, and he set it down on the table.

"Thanks. We'll have to eat that later."

She smiled at his father and put the pudding in the fridge. Meanwhile, his father ushered them into the living room.

Once they were settled on the couch, Sakuta's mother asked, "Are you staying for dinner? I'll have to add a dish or two and reprep the rice cooker."

"No..."

But before Sakuta could insist they weren't staying long, Mai got to her feet.

"I'll help," she said, joining his mother in the kitchen.

"Oh? You don't mind?" She seemed unsure she should really let the famous actress help.

"I wanna learn the secrets to 'Mom's cooking,'" Mai insisted.

"Golly, it's like you two are newlyweds already!"

His mother looked pretty pleased and got an apron out for Mai. They started peeling potatoes together, talking about Sakuta as they worked. Mai always acted a tad more formal around his parents, which was a strange feeling.

But he was glad to see her building a good relationship with them.

He'd first introduced her to his mother in March this year. He'd come over to tell them he'd passed his exams and gotten into college, and he'd brought Mai with him.

With Kaede doing better, their mother had stabilized, and he'd hoped it would be safe to start pushing the boundaries.

But it still came as quite a surprise. Mai Sakurajima was a household name. And his mother had been watching her act since she was a tiny child. Having someone like that show up as your son's girlfriend made it hard to act normal.

Sakuta's father had told her about Mai, of course, and that likely helped her keep it together.

But she'd definitely spent several minutes dreamily going, "It's really true! It really is. You're really…just as beautiful."

And since then, they'd come over to visit on several other occasions.

"Coming from school?" his father asked, lowering the volume on the news. He was trying his best to be hospitable.

"Basically."

The screen was already showing early Christmas illumination news.

"Don't suppose you two remember the Akagis at all?" Sakuta asked.

Mai's eyes snapped to him. She was probably wondering if this was safe to bring up around his mother.

She'd been unable to find a way to help Kaede with her bullies, felt like she was a failure of a mother, and had a breakdown. It had been bad enough she couldn't live a normal life afterward.

But that was no longer the case. Kaede, Sakuta, their mom, and their dad had all gotten through the hard times and were able to spend time together as a family again.

And seeing how much Kaede was enjoying life gave their mother mental fortitude.

Knowing Sakuta was having fun with his amazing girlfriend gave her confidence.

She'd happily said as much herself.

So he was pretty sure she could handle this much.

And he was right.

Neither of his parents batted an eye.

"The Akagis? Yes, I remember them. They had a daughter, right?"

"Mm."

"I believe her mother was a lawyer."

That was news to him. Maybe Ikumi's serious/righteous thing came from her mother's legal experience.

"And I'm pretty sure she was on the PTA," his dad added.

"That's right! Managing that alongside work is something else."

It sounded like her mother also never took time off. In high school, Akagi had been class president and volunteered; now she was going to nursing school *and* playing hero.

"But what brought that on?" his mother asked, eyes on her cooking.

"Akagi goes to our college. Different major, but I bumped into her recently. I didn't remember her at all, so I was just wondering what she was like."

"Then I've got just the thing."

"Mm?"

His father stood up, opened the sliding door, and vanished into a bedroom. He came back with an album in a crisp paper case.

"……"

He held it out to Sakuta.

It was quite heavy.

"Is this…?"

He didn't really have to ask.

The term had already floated into his mind.

His graduation album.

"Found it with the winter things."

He took it out of the case.

The cover bore the name of his junior high.

Not exactly a trip down memory lane.

He'd never even seen the graduation album before.

He didn't even remember opening it once. Had likely never taken it out of the case it came in.

Brand-new, consigned to the junk drawer.

But somehow, it had ended up back in his hands.

"The moving men spotted it and double-checked if we really wanted to throw it out."

"……"

"I assumed you might not want it now, but at some point in the future, you might change your mind."

"Maybe…," Sakuta said. He opened to the first page.

Left fallow for years, the album was stiff, the pages plastered to each other. Each page he turned made tearing noises.

He stopped at the page for Class 3-1.

Sakuta's glum face was at the front of the class.

Azusagawa, always the first in line.

Ikumi was at the front of the girls' side, looking collected.

Akagi was also always first.

That jogged a few memories.

Sakuta and Ikumi had sat next to each other at the start of their third year. Each first in their row.

He turned another page. The smell of ink and paper wafted off the album and down his nostrils. It felt like a trip down memory lane, even if these weren't the memories he wanted. His body reacted instinctively, like this was stamped into his DNA.

Past the sections on each class, he found a collage of school activity photos. All the students looked fresh-faced at the entrance ceremony. Hyped up at a sports festival. Excitedly showing off culture festival costumes. There were pictures of sporting leagues and field trips.

Everyone was having fun. Like the three years they spent together had been a blast.

There wasn't a single glimpse of the gray misery he'd lived through. It was all vivid colors. This album was a lie.

He turned more pages, and the pictures gave way to black-and-white text.

Two essays per page, one from a boy, one from a girl. Class 3-1's first page had Sakuta Azusagawa's and Ikumi Akagi's names side by side at the top.

Living Up to My Ideals

Ikumi Akagi, Class 3-1

For my elementary school graduation essay, I wrote that I wanted to grow up to be someone who helps others. At the time, I thought junior high school students *were* grown-ups, but now that I'm graduating, I know I've fallen far short of my goals.

I was class president my first year and did my part to help prep and manage the sports and culture festivals. The latter especially—I stayed so late the teachers brought us food, and I know that was worth it. They're fond memories now.

My second year was all about the student council. I was appointed secretary, and every task that came my way was a new experience. I was in contact with every club and every student government position. I made a ton of friends outside my class and outside my year. I cannot begin to express how grateful I am for the time we spent together.

But in my third year, I failed to do anything.

In high school, I hope this time I really will grow up and really will become someone who helps others.

This was a very formulaic essay.

An expression of her earnest, dedicated personality.

And that's exactly why the one line devoted to her last year high-lighted how intense her regrets were.

She'd likely had more to say.

Maybe she'd even written it.

Perhaps her teacher had edited it down to that line after submission. The simple phrasing that survived stuck with him.

Maybe he was overthinking it, but Sakuta doubted that very much.

——*I failed to do anything.*

Anyone who was in that class would know exactly what she was talking about and when.

He'd been right. She did regret it.

Regretted not helping him.

And she was still carrying that. The fact that she remembered what she'd written in her graduation essay proved it.

Perhaps in her mind, she'd made a point of writing that line down in her album as a form of self-reproach.

Most people would soon forget what they'd written. Sakuta sure had.

——*I'd like to reach a place of kindness.*

At the campus festival, Ikumi had thrown that line back at him, and it hadn't rung a bell. Had he really written that? He still wasn't sure.

Sakuta's own essay was right here, at the top of the page.

Maybe that would jog his memory. With that in mind, he struggled to make out his terrible junior high handwriting.

The contents were as messy as his penmanship. It was clear he'd been told to write *something* and had forced the words out.

As empty as the essay might be, it was worth struggling through.

No matter how many times he reread it, the line wasn't there. He hadn't written that. Hadn't written *I'd like to reach a place of kindness.*

A tremor ran through him. He felt downright dizzy.

Sakuta hadn't written those words.

But they reminded him of something.

A treasured concept taught to him by his first love.

How had Ikumi known about it?

His swirling thoughts began to gather, coalescing into an answer.

"If she…"

And the very idea sent a chill through him.

It was probably dead on.

He felt sure of it.

Yet that didn't bring him any comfort. Quite the opposite.

Sakuta had finally found the answer he was looking for, but he was just as lost as before.

Chapter

4

From Deep in the Hilbert space

1

The lunch rush died down around three PM. The restaurant's bustle gave way to the usual relaxed vibe. The seats went from full up to half capacity.

He thought he might be able to bow out soon.

No sooner had the thought crossed his mind than his manager said, "Azusagawa, you can clock out."

"Don't mind if I do," he said, and he headed to the break room, where the time cards were.

He was greeted by the rear end of a high school girl peering into the staff fridge. She was in full ostrich mode.

"Koga, that is too much butt."

Tomoe righted herself immediately, putting both hands over the back of her skirt.

"You are the *worst*."

She puffed out her cheeks, glaring at him. She clearly intended to look angry, but it was more like a chipmunk with its cheeks full of acorns. Possibly a pudgy hamster. Either way, not threatening. Just adorable.

"Those are the cream puffs I owe you."

"I said one would be plenty!" she grumbled, pulling the white box out of the fridge. It was a bit big to hold one-handed, and it had ten cream puffs inside.

Sakuta had swung by the cream puff shop by the JR Fujisawa Station gates on his way here. Tomoe's shift started after his, so he'd put a note on the fridge door that said, *Koga's cream puffs—do not eat.*

"And this note!" she yelled, snatching it off the door and shoving it in his face. "The others were all laughing at me! 'Can you really eat *all* of those?'"

"You can share the rest if you like. Kaede's coming later on."

"Then write *For everyone*!"

"This is funnier."

He took the note from her, balled it up, and tossed it in the wastebasket.

"I disagree," Tomoe said, opening the box. The smell of maple syrup filled the room. "They look so good!"

With that, she bit into one. The sweet cream banished her irritation, and a happy smile spread across her cheeks.

Sakuta seized that chance to duck behind the lockers. These were tall enough to scrape the ceiling and neatly split the room in two, giving the male staff a makeshift changing room.

He stripped out of his server apron, shirt, and slacks, down to his underwear.

"Oh yeah, Koga," he said, calling over the lockers.

"Mmph?"

"You know about the dreaming hashtag?"

"You only *just* found out?"

Koga was a very modern schoolgirl, always on top of the latest trends, and this was old news to her.

"As a prophetic dreams trendsetter, what's your take?"

"I think it's kinda creepy."

"It ain't much compared with your future simulation, true."

The petite devil's version absolutely destroyed these dreams. Her simulation had let him experience a whole future month in real time.

"I'm not competing!"

"But you don't think they're fake."

"Yeah, well…"

That sounded evasive.

"Did you have one yourself?"

"Not personally, but Nana's dream came true."

That was her friend Nana Yoneyama.

"What kind?"

"A boy hit on me at the beach."

She sounded loath to admit it.

"When was that?"

"End of July."

Today was November 27. This was four whole months ago. No wonder she'd been surprised he brought it up. The hashtag had been around for ages.

"Come to think of it, I didn't get to see you in a swimsuit this year."

"Or the year before!"

"Oh, I see. You buy a new one every year, then? Looking forward to next year's, then."

"I did *not* say that."

"But you must get hit on all the time."

"The boy in question was the same one Nana saw in her dream, which is the only reason I'm telling you about this at all."

He didn't need to see her face to picture how cross she must look. Maybe she'd better eat a second cream puff.

"What happened to the boy?"

"He's dating Nana now."

"Oh?"

That was a shocking twist.

"He went to the same junior high as her."

If that alone was a basis for dating, Sakuta and Ikumi would have hooked up by now.

"Did they have a thing for each other at the time?"

"Nana did, apparently. Don't think he did. He seemed pretty sur-prised that was her."

"Ah. You did sort of transform her."

Nana stopped by the restaurant every couple of months, so Sakuta saw her often enough.

When they'd first met, she was a quiet, reserved first-year. Two years later, she'd had quite the glow up.

She hadn't changed herself overnight (like Tomoe's pre–high school makeover), but a boy who'd missed the steps in between would cer-tainly find it shocking. She was simply much cuter now.

By this point, Sakuta was dressed again, and he came back into the break room.

Tomoe had finished her cream puff and was folding up the wrapper. She looked a bit put out.

"Are you that shocked Yoneyama got out ahead of you?"

"Th-that's not the problem! I mean, last week when she said they were going out now, it was certainly surprising, but… I dunno, I'm just feeling pressured."

"That's totally a Koga problem."

"What that's supposed to mean?"

He'd meant it was straightforward and genuine, but he didn't want to admit that. He figured she wouldn't take it as a compliment. And he could tell she already knew what he meant. That's why she was mad at him.

"Just don't rush into dating some weirdo," he said.

"There aren't too many people weirder than you, Senpai. I'm safe."

"Well, thanks a lot."

He put a little box on her head.

"Stop it—you'll ruin my hair," she grumbled, reaching for it. She set the box down on the table and blinked at it. "Uh, Senpai? Is this…?"

The box contained the latest in wireless earphones. When he'd asked what to get her to celebrate college admission, she'd mentioned these.

"I haven't even told you the referral results yet!"

"You managed to get a referral retracted? That'd honestly be impressive."

Colleges had a set number of referrals per high school, so they were almost always a guaranteed admission. Unless you totally blew your interview.

"I—I got in."

"Then congrats. As promised."

"You're sure? These aren't cheap."

"I used a secret art that ensured not one yen left my wallet."

"You what?"

"I ask Zukki, and she just gave me them. One of every color, so I got extras."

These were the earphones Uzuki had done a commercial for.

"And I can just have them?"

"I told Zukki they were to celebrate a kohai's college admission. She knows I don't have a phone and can't exactly use them myself."

"Oh. Well, I guess that's okay."

"Don't party too hard."

"Nana's still studying, so I can't party even if I want to. But thanks."

Tomoe opened the box, took out the earphones, and tried to link them to her phone. Midway she went, "Oh, right," and looked up. "That reminds me…"

"What?"

"I saw a worrying post yesterday. About our high school."

Tomoe glanced back at her phone and scrolled down her feed.

"Right, this one."

She lifted her head and showed him the tweet in question.

——Had a dream I was injured by a broken light bulb in class. Ouch. November 27, Minegahara High, Class 2-1. Probably changing after practice. Probably shouldn't throw basketballs around indoors… #dreaming

That was worrying.

But Sakuta wasn't—he knew this was a fake. He'd written it himself. He'd made a whole new account to do so.

"That one's fine."

"How so?"

"A hero will handle it."

Ikumi would show up for sure. He was laying bait for her.

"Senpai, have you finally lost it?"

There was a look of genuine concern in her eyes.

He objected to that in principle, but explaining the whole thing would take too long. He had places to be. Catching up with that hero.

"Afternoon, everyone," Kaede said, coming into the break room.

"Oh, hey, Kaede."

"Hi, Tomoe!"

Kaede's smile faded when she turned to Sakuta.

"Rio's waiting for you outside," she said.

"Right on time."

The clock in the break room said 3:20.

"I'm outta here."

"Oh, okay. Have fun! Kaede, want a cream puff?"

"Oooh! You bet!"

"I think I got room for a second."

Laughing at that, Sakuta left the break room.

True to Kaede's word, Rio was standing outside the restaurant.

Alone by a lamppost.

"Thanks for waiting. And coming."

"I was here for a class anyway."

She started walking.

Sakuta matched her pace.

This road ran directly to the station, but the private lesson–based cram school they worked at was on the way.

"First, about Ikumi Akagi's Adolescence Syndrome—your suggestion's on the money, Azusagawa. That seems the most likely possibility."

He'd called Rio after seeing the graduation album. Their schedules hadn't quiet lined up, and he was only just now getting to pick her brain further.

"Though it is rather hard to believe."

"Agreed."

Sakuta found his own idea difficult to swallow.

"If I was in the same position, I couldn't do what she is."

"Me neither."

If Sakuta was right, then Ikumi's Adolescence Syndrome was already active during the college entrance ceremony. And she'd been in the throes of it ever since—at least eight months.

Presumably, she'd made the conscious choice to keep the symptoms going.

That was hard to believe, but if Rio had reached the same verdict, then he had to trust his own conclusion.

"If there's a 'first,' you've got more?"

Rio had begun with that word.

But what she'd said after that was all he'd wanted from her.

"Watch the road for me."

Without waiting for an answer, Rio took out her phone.

"Okay, okay."

She started tapping the screen. Sakuta's job was to keep her from bumping into oncoming pedestrians.

A good thirty seconds later, she said, "This," and showed him her screen.

It was a social media post.

He spotted the dreaming hashtag right away.

The date—was November 27.

Posted at the start of the month.

——**November 27, went to my junior high reunion. If that actually happens, I'll freak. #dreaming**

"There's, like, ten more of these."

She typed something else in and showed him the results.

——**November 27, Sunday. Reunion at a seaside shop. Maybe junior high? But everyone having fun. Huge shock. Will this come true? #dreaming**

——**November 27. Was that a reunion dream? Could see Osanbashi from the shop. Like, everyone looked believably aged up, might really come true? Doubt it. #dreaming**

——**November 27, I think. Hear we're doing a junior high reunion and dreamed about it that night. Same shop as the invite. Might be real! But with that class? Still, looked like fun. Should I go? #dreaming**

Every date matched.

From what he could tell from the profiles, the posters were Sakuta's age. Their profiles had hints of their colleges or locations, and all of them were local.

Coincidence. Overthinking it.

He could have assumed that but felt disinclined.

"This got anything to do with you?"

"It might. I do have an invite."

He took the postcard-sized flyer out of his rucksack's pouch and showed it to her. It was the one Ikumi had given him.

A reunion party on November 27. Two whole hours, from four to six. In the Yokohama Bay area. Right near the Osanbashi Pier.

The vibe of the shop was just like the posts described.

"Ikumi Akagi had a dream about this, too?"

"The one where she hurt someone."

Seiichi Takasaka, her ex, had told him about it. He'd found the post on an account he was pretty sure belonged to her.

"Is it a coincidence so many hashtag dreaming posts are about this?"

"That's what I wanna know."

"Well, if you've taken steps, I'm not gonna worry, but…"

Rio stopped. They were outside the cram school.

"But?"

"Try to be careful."

"Of what?"

"It might be you she stabs."

With that, she headed inside.

"……"

He hadn't really considered that possibility.

"…Maybe I should tuck a magazine under my shirt."

He glanced at the periodicals rack and saw a fashion magazine with Mai's face on the front next to a *shounen* manga magazine with Sweet Bullet smiling on the cover.

2

It had been ages since Sakuta had ridden the Enoden, and it felt familiar—but also like he no longer belonged there.

He'd ridden this train on a daily basis all through high school.

Taken the slow rolling scenery for granted.

Got used to seeing the car thread its way through the houses.

The old-timey sounds of the cars, the rails, and the connectors rattling.

It had all been part of his routine.

And now it no longer was.

Since starting college, he'd barely even gone to the south side of Fujisawa Station, where the Enoden platform lay. He hadn't even noticed that until today.

Both the restaurant and cram school were on the north end, and the grocery store and his apartment were, too. He never needed the other side.

For that reason, when they pulled out of Enoshima Station, his eyes were glued to the scenery. Even through Koshigoe, he was still gaping at the houses, walls, and trees that seemed ready to bang up against the sides of the car.

The scenery itself was so close you could almost reach out and touch it. He got worried again that they actually would bump something, but then the tracks hit Route 134, and the whole side of the train turned blue.

The sun was headed down the sky to the west, and it made the waters gleam.

The sky hung overhead, blue and white as far as the eye could see.

The horizon seemed to glow.

He'd seen this every day in high school.

Had gazed absently out the windows at it.

But that was no ordinary commute.

Now that he was in college, that fact was driven home.

——*"Next stop, Shichirigahama."*

He hadn't heard that female announcer's voice in ages, either.

He disembarked on the tiny platform at Shichirigahama and found it so quiet it was like he'd been spit out into an empty world. The Enoden car itself had been full enough, but barely anyone else got off or on here. It was that time of day.

But it didn't feel lonely. Quite the opposite. The moment he stepped off the train, the smell of the ocean wrapped him in its warm embrace. The memories came rushing into his nostrils, raced through his circulatory system, and filled him with the comfort of home. His very cells remembering what it had been like here.

He tapped his commuter pass on the reader at the gate and left the station.

Not long after, he saw his old school across a little bridge.

For three whole years, he'd gone to Minegahara High.

Everyone else from his train turned down the gentle slope to the ocean. Sakuta alone went the other way, up the hill and through the railroad crossing.

Beyond that lay the Minegahara school gates.

They were half-open, and Sakuta took a deep breath before stepping through.

He'd never stressed about it like this when he was a student here.

After graduating, he was an outsider.

And it was weird to walk around the grounds in street clothes.

Fortunately, it was a Sunday, and there were no signs of any students. There were probably people here for practice or clubs, but he reached the building without encountering any.

He swung by the office first.

He could hear sounds of ball dribbling on the basketball courts now. He knocked at the glass window, calling to see if anyone was there.

A woman came out to greet him.

"You're the graduate who called ahead?"

"Yep. Sakuta Azusagawa."

"Then just put your name here."

He went to write his name and saw another on the ledger above.

——*Ikumi Akagi.*

The time written next to it was 3:40. Fifteen minutes ago. Today's date.

"Oh, her? A college student, wanted to look around the building. Material for a college report."

"Ah," he said. He'd given a similar fake reason when securing permission to visit.

He wrote his name.

"Try not to take pictures that can identify any individuals, please."

"Right."

"And wear this while you're here."

She handed him a visitor's lanyard.

"Bring that back when you're done."

"Got it."

He hung the lanyard around his neck.

"Should be less than an hour," he said, and with that, he headed upstairs.

The school interior on a weekend didn't jog any memories.

The deserted silence won out, and the vibe was too different to take him back.

The only sound was his slippers padding up the stairs.

Sakuta took it one step at a time and was soon on the second floor.

The hall ran straight ahead. Nothing blocked his view. No one was around. White signs were near the ceiling, from Class 2-1 all the way to 2-9.

Nothing different. It had been less than a year since he'd graduated, so what even would change?

But he could feel it on his skin. He no longer belonged here.

It was very uncomfortable. He'd gotten permission but felt guilty anyway.

But he had bigger fish to fry. He hadn't come here to explore his alma mater.

All classroom doors were closed.

But when he looked carefully, one was open a crack.

The rear door of Class 2-1.

Sakuta's class, once.

He'd sat in there for a whole year.

He started walking toward the open door.

And went right on in.

"……"

He stopped just inside the door, spotting the person who had beat him there.

She was standing by the windows near the front row. Her street clothes looked out of place in the classroom. There was no mistaking her.

That was Ikumi.

She must have noticed his entrance.

With each step he took, the silly sound of his slippers echoed through the room.

Sakuta headed straight across the room from the back door and stopped at the windows over the coast. He undid the lock and opened the window. The chill ocean breeze brushed his cheeks.

That sensation sure took him back.

When he'd had the window seat, he'd spent a lot of time absently gazing out the window. Somehow he never grew tired of this view. The ocean was just compelling that way.

"You've always regretted it, Akagi."

"……"

Ikumi said nothing, even when he spoke. Just kept staring at the sea.

"Baffling cuts and bruises all over Kaede, and I just wanted the teachers and my classmates to believe me, to do something to help us."

Both knew the outcome. No one had believed his story. Neither staff nor students had extended a helping hand.

All they'd done was whisper "Azusagawa's lost it!" or "He's gone mad!" or bore into him with horrified stares.

"You regret not being able to help me."

What had actually saved him were the fuzzy memories of a mysterious high school girl who appeared in his dreams. Memories of his first love, carved into his soul. Those had been his beacon.

"Not…quite," Ikumi said as she turned his way.

"Oh?"

"I regret being unable to do anything when my friends came to me like, 'Ikumi, do something about this grim mood!'"

"……"

"Even as a kid, people said I had my head on straight and could be relied on. Parents, teachers, friends. I felt like I could do anything."

She'd definitely had her act together more than others her age. She'd had prior successes. Until that year, she'd lived up to people's expectations. Ikumi had never faced a challenge she wasn't a match for. She'd done the work and come through.

But that mess in junior high was too much for anyone.

Kaede's bullying, Adolescence Syndrome, dissociative disorder—none of those were problems a single third-year junior high student was capable of solving.

Those weren't burdens she should have been asked to bear.

But Ikumi wasn't hiding behind that. She never had and still wasn't.

"That tripped me up, and…I think I never really recovered from it. I still haven't righted myself."

That earnest streak had almost certainly caused her own Adolescence Syndrome. She was too forthright, too tenacious, too harsh on herself. That had become *her*.

"You lured me out here to take this trip down memory lane? With that fake post?"

"Glad nobody's hurt?"

"Yeah. But make this the last one. I've missed the reunion now."

Ikumi turned back to the water.

The clock on the wall showed four. The reunion party was starting. The organizers would be making speeches any minute.

"I thought you weren't up for hearing the other girls brag about their boyfriends?"

"I *was* class rep. Figured I should do my part."

Very her.

"But when you think about it, this *is* a class reunion. The classroom means a lot."

"To you, Azusagawa."

She rolled her eyes at him.

It was a clear message that wasn't true for *her*.

But it was.

He knew that now.

He'd figured it out.

That's why he'd chosen to have their talk here.

"And you, Akagi."

"……"

That simple phrase made her eyes waver. She seemed lost in thought. Her gaze searched his face for answers. Whatever was going through her head, her lips parted slightly, but she said nothing. Like she feared anything she did say would play right into his hand.

Sakuta *had* been trying to fish the words out of her.

But if she didn't take the bait, he had a backup plan. He would have to cut to the heart of things. Talk was free.

"You were part of this class, Akagi. In the other potential world."

"……"

No response from her. She was just gazing at the expanse of water, blinking at a natural speed. Didn't seem surprised. Didn't laugh off his words, either.

At length, she inhaled.

"I remember this breeze," she murmured, to no one in particular.

The ocean breeze played with Ikumi's hair. She put up a hand to hold it still.

"The smell of the sea, the line of the horizon…"

Like her, Sakuta's eyes were on the water. He could sense her standing next to him.

"It hasn't changed at all. It seems so long ago."

They'd graduated and were in college now. It was the two of them who'd changed. That's why it felt like a memory. Even though it was just a year ago, the view of the sea, sky, and horizon had always been there. That routine now felt extraordinary.

And their lives here now a thing of the past.

"How'd you know?"

She was bathed in the light of the setting sun, and the wind caught her voice.

"Something felt off when we saw each other at the entrance ceremony."

"……"

"You took the trouble to call out to me then, Akagi. But not a word since."

And in hindsight, that was kinda odd.

"I admit—it didn't really bug me until recent events."

Sakuta had just shaken it off and gone about his new life. Wasn't compelled to approach her himself and hadn't needed to.

"But after Halloween?"

"Yep. That made me start to wonder about things."

"Like…?"

"Why you and Kamisato are close."

Two people he knew had connected when he wasn't looking. Was that just a coincidence? That Ikumi/Saki pairing sure felt like more than that to him. They were a bit too tight to have first met in college.

"We were in the same class in high school the last two years."

That was the other world. In this one, Ikumi had never gone to Minegahara High. They'd never once shared a class.

"When we first bumped into each other, I called her Saki, and she looked weirded out. My first big blunder since arriving here. I managed to play it off as mistaking her for a friend. And we did end up talking more."

A smile passed across her lips.

"Then there's the boyfriend thing. I didn't think that was real, but he exists."

"This Saki was all, "Ikumi, you have got to get at least one boy in your life.'"

The way she acted around guys did not seem like someone who had dating experience. At the very least, she didn't seem like someone who'd lived with a boyfriend and looked after him.

"And there's the poltergeist," Sakuta said.

"……"

"Most people would freak out after running into the supernatural."

But Ikumi had taken it in stride and hadn't seemed remotely scared. Because she knew for a fact it was harmless.

"That's sensory feedback from the Akagi who went to the other world?"

All those sensations were supposed to be in this world. That's why they manifested themselves here, through the conduit of her body. Rio had backed that notion up.

"And the writing on your arm is from the other Akagi?"

That also explained how Ikumi was acting. It came from *her*. Another Ikumi, who hailed from a different potential world. That's why she was fine with it. That's why she'd laughed it off. It was all *her*.

"……"

She wasn't shaking her head. Instead, she asked, "This is all pure conjecture?"

"The clincher was finding the graduation album."

The final answer she was searching for. With this, everything added up.

"You said you threw it out."

"And I did. But the movers found it and slipped it to my dad behind my back."

Keeping that fact from Sakuta was just grown-ups being considerate. If he'd known, he definitely would've thrown it out again.

"Wish they hadn't."

She would. Being nice to one person might not be nice to someone else. This had helped Sakuta but was actively causing trouble for her.

"You mentioned what I wrote in my essay, right?"

"You want to reach a place of kindness."

She threw the words up to the sky above.

"But I didn't write that."

At the time, he still hadn't fully recovered memories of Shouko. He'd had dreams about a strange high school girl—but that was it. Dreams he could barely even remember.

The other Sakuta had likely remembered both Shouko and Makinohara sooner. While still in junior high. And that's why he'd left their message behind in his graduation essay. He'd probably solved Kaede's problems faster, too.

"I'm not as good at this stuff as that other Sakuta."

That earned him a smile. It was also acknowledgment that he was right.

The two worlds were pretty similar, but they had their differences. For both Sakuta and Ikumi. They were the same people but not exactly alike. And those small differences had led to major discrepancies.

Like Sakuta being better at stuff and Ikumi going to Minegahara.

"Can't believe you kept a straight face."

The entrance ceremony had been ages back. Eight months ago. And Ikumi had been in this world the whole time. Still was.

"I'm a lot more comfortable on this side."

"Even though I suck now?"

"Yes."

He'd been half joking, but that nod was far more than half-serious.

"You read my graduation essay?" she asked.

"The one about growing up to help people?"

"I didn't pull that off in the other world."

"Too soon to give up."

She'd barely started college. But if she was saying she hadn't pulled it off, there must have been a reason for that. And the main reason there…

"I can't compete with the better Sakuta," she said.

"……"

"You didn't let me do anything in junior high."

"Then…"

"When the bullies came for your sister, you handled it all yourself."

In that world, at least.

"High school didn't slow you down. You saved Sakurajima, Koga, Futaba… All the problems I wanted to help with, you fixed them all alone."

"……"

"Azusagawa, you were what I wanted to be."

If his memories really had come back in junior high, then it made sense he'd have been so proactive it spooked her.

His time with Shouko had really done a number on his personality. It was the foundation of his being. It had made him grow up.

And it also meant he knew things about the future. Without that knowledge, Ikumi couldn't compete. Sakuta had been cheating.

"Three whole years of high school, and I didn't become anything. I just festered, envying you."

"……"

"I even failed my college exams. I couldn't even become a college student, much less someone who mattered. Nothing went right. I spent all my time wanting to escape, to be somewhere else."

"And you wound up in this world?"

Ikumi nodded slowly.

"The first thing I knew, I was on campus…and saw you there."

——*"You are Azusagawa, right?"*

——*"Akagi?"*

——*"Yeah. Been a while."*

That was the moment. Nodoka and Uzuki had come up behind him, and they hadn't spoken further.

"I thought I was dreaming."

"Naturally."

Sakuta had thought the same.

"But I wasn't. I knew because I'd met you in my world."

Her eyes were locked on his.

"……"

"You came to visit in winter of our second year."

He had *not* expected her to realize that.

"You noticed?"

"I watched you pretty close."

That was not a sweet sentiment. Just…forlorn.

"The next day, you didn't remember what we'd talked about. I always thought that was weird."

And coming to a new world herself resolved the doubt. And that realization had provided the impetus for her to accept the fact that she was in a new potential world. Perhaps that had led to her believing in Adolescence Syndrome.

"Well, sorry. That one's all on me. Not the other Sakuta's fault at all."

"No, I'm actually grateful. It might well be I was only able to reach this world because of what you did."

Honestly, he wasn't sure if the two things were related. But it was possible his own visit had left a path between the worlds. To borrow Rio's phrasing, Sakuta's perceptions had locked the two worlds to their current forms.

"…You didn't want to go back?"

"I didn't, and I still don't."

No hesitation.

"……"

"Here, I'm a student at the college I wanted to go to. I'm the rep for a volunteer group. And…"

"The hero thing."

Ikumi made a face. Like being in college meant they'd outgrown those ideas.

"In this world, I'm the person I wanted to be."

So she didn't want to go back. Didn't need to go back. The occasional poltergeist attack wasn't that big a deal.

The life she led in this world was just that fulfilling. She was the ideal she'd failed to become back where she came from.

She'd played the hero's role to perfection. Even at the festival, she'd just been relieved to hear no one would actually be hurt.

Ikumi's choices were consistent.

But not when it came to him. There, her actions didn't add up. Still weren't, right now.

"So why'd you make a bet with me?"

If she wanted to protect her new life, she should have just pushed him away. He was the only person capable of figuring out her lie. A fact so simple she had to know it.

"I thought I could actually beat you in this world."

This, too, came straight from the heart.

"Then why did losing the bet come as a relief?" he asked, looking right at her.

At her unruffled expression.

"Because..."

Ikumi broke off. She was bad at lying, so no lies came to mind.

"......"

He waited awhile, but she said nothing else.

"You wanted someone to notice?"

"......"

She held his gaze.

"Someone to know you weren't the real Ikumi Akagi."

"...Why do you think that?"

A whisper, carried on the breeze.

Ikumi meant every word she'd said here today.

She liked being in this world.

Here, she was who she wanted to be.

Her life was fulfilling.

So she wanted to stay.

Not a word of that was false.

Had it not been Ikumi, that would have been the end of it. But unfortunately, she *was* Ikumi Akagi.

The same girl who'd written *I want to be someone who helps others* in her graduation essay. A lofty goal.

No way she didn't have doubts.

"You're too harsh on yourself to just run away."

That was why she'd wanted someone to catch her cheating.

Even as she enjoyed her new life, part of her had always felt guilty for it.

Deep down, she'd known she couldn't keep doing this.

The closer she got to her ideals, the more she enjoyed her life…the more that guilt ballooned within.

Honest to a fault, unable to live any other way.

That was who Ikumi Akagi was.

"So I guess that means…gotcha, Akagi."

Ikumi had not taken her eyes off him once. She was still maintaining eye contact. Her eyes had grown moist, and when she blinked, tears rolled down her cheeks.

"I was always good at hide-and-seek," she said, her voice choked up. "But I didn't think I could hide here forever."

She *would* feel that way.

"But nobody noticed. No one caught me. I started losing track of who I even was. I'm not even the Ikumi Akagi they think they know. Everyone just *thinks* I'm her. I'm not her, but it's like it's fine if I am."

Most people wouldn't figure that out. How could they? They might think something seemed off or ask what was wrong, but it wouldn't provoke anything beyond an initial sense of concern. How would anyone guess you were actually from a different potential world?

If peaceful college life were interrupted by accusations like that, everyone would think the accuser was a total weirdo. Even if they were right. Common sense would support everyone else and make an enemy of the odd man out. The world would be against them. Lynched by an invisible force existing only in society as made by and for humans.

"If the replacement me will do, then who even am I? I've been wondering that all along."

"Did this get you any closer?"

"No. Not at all."

Ikumi's eyes turned to him for help.

"Akagi, you want it all, and you want to handle it all yourself," he said, eyes on the ocean.

"......"

"It's almost funny how serious you are. Really helps pull off the nurse costume."

Outside the window, the sun was setting. Disappearing behind Enoshima.

"That's who you are."

"That's it?" she scoffed. "A few years from now, it won't be a costume."

"Then I'll have to update it to 'looks great in her uniform.'"

With the way she was bathed in the golden light, he could no longer see any tears.

3

They swung by the office, then left the school. The sky had given way to night.

Sakuta's footsteps brought him toward the gate, and Ikumi's followed alongside.

"We walked like this that day," she said, facing forward.

She must have been talking about the day he'd spent in her world. His first time meeting this Ikumi.

"Do you remember what we talked about?"

"You yelled at me for not turning in the class log."

"I was *helping*."

Not yelling. She laughed.

"It was reasonably intimidating."

"…Still, I'm surprised you remembered me."

"Meeting you then is why I remembered. Like, oh yeah, she was in my third-year class."

That was how fuzzy his memories of her had been. He'd only formed a clear picture of who Ikumi Akagi was in that other world.

If he hadn't met Ikumi there, even if she'd called out to him that first day here, he'd never have dug up her name. He'd have had to go, "Who are you again?"

"So I guess you made an impact on me."

"……"

Ikumi said nothing else. Like she had that day, she just walked quietly next to him. But they had said things then. Enough that she would ask about it.

"What did you almost say to me?"

——"*Azusagawa…*"

She'd called his name, looking tense.

Her eyes turned his way for a moment, like she'd steeled her nerves.

"Seems like you've forgotten what I said next."

"You just said, 'Never mind.'"

Weird to remember her deciding not to say a thing.

"Did you say the rest to the other me?"

"If I'd finished the line then, what would you have done?"

Ikumi seemed a little unsure of herself.

"I'd have been pretty chuffed."

"…Even with your amazing girlfriend?"

"I ain't popular enough to get sick of confessions."

"You just can't answer a question straight, can you?"

"Like you do."

She laughed.

They were both deflecting. Most of their conversations were like that.

"Is there a point in asking someone out when you know the answer?" Ikumi asked.

"A while back, I had someone I lost track of without saying my piece. I went after them but couldn't find them anywhere. And I wished I'd said it while I still could."

"So you think I should?"

"That's just how it worked for me."

He couldn't say what was best for her. All he could say was how he'd felt about it when it was his turn.

"…Well, I'll bear that in mind," she said, after a long, thoughtful silence.

That was a very Ikumi response.

"If the other Sakuta's better, you can say whatever."

He'd probably handle it well.

"Say what you feel. Love, hate, frustration, I'm sick of your goddamn face—you know, whatever."

"Should I tell him this was your idea?"

"Go right ahead."

He'd never meet the other Sakuta. They were unable to coexist on a quantum level. Rio had explained that principle once.

They left the gates behind and moved to the railroad crossing. As if it had been waiting for them, the bells started ringing, warning of the next train's approach.

He could see a train slowly rounding the curve from Kamakura, bound for Fujisawa Station. If he was headed home, he'd want to catch that train—or be stuck waiting more than ten minutes.

His high school years had ingrained that habit, and he started walking fast. He made it across the tracks before the gates dropped.

But Ikumi was no longer with him.

He turned back and found her standing on the far side of the crossing. Only five or six yards away. A few steps. But the path was already blocked.

"This is good-bye," she said, yelling over the bells.

"You're sure?" he said, calling back.

"I feel ready."

Her smile was genuine, like she'd accomplished something. A much brighter expression than anything he'd seen in the classroom. Sakuta wasn't sure what that meant, or what the word *ready* implied.

"What…?" But before he could ask—

"Message from the other me," Ikumi said, bending down. She grabbed the left cuff of her wide-leg pants and pulled it way up, revealing her entire leg.

The pale skin of her thigh.

Something written on it in black marker.

——*Waiting at the reunion.*

He was even more confused. But even as his head spun, he felt a wave of panic rising. Maybe this *wasn't* over yet. If there was still a chance she'd hurt someone—

And the look on her face confirmed that fear.

She'd seen his expression—and smiled.

"You saw that post?"

The train was almost here. He could barely hear her.

"What's your plan, Akagi?!" he yelled.

But all he got in return was her mouthing, "Good-bye."

A moment later, the train from Kamakura hit the crossing. It rolled slowly between Sakuta and Ikumi.

A four-car train, two cars of one design, the others of another. That felt very long right now. The noise of bells added to his fretting, rising up through the soles of his feet. The stress squeezed his body. Each time there was a gap in the train, he tried to catch a glimpse of the other side, but it was too brief to make out much of anything.

That repeated three times, and finally, the train cleared the crossing.

And the view opened up again.

"......?!"

He'd anticipated it. Seen it coming.

And it was just like he'd expected. Ikumi was gone.

Yet his body still reeled with shock. New questions poured into his mind.

"......"

An entirely different girl stood where Ikumi had been.

The bells stopped.

The gates lifted.

And the knapsack kid walked over the crossing, careful not to get her feet caught in the rails.

He knew this kid.

She looked just like the child actress Mai Sakurajima.

Sakuta knew instinctively this was the same girl he'd met before.

The one who'd taken him to that other potential world.

But she'd grown up since then.

When they'd first met, she'd looked to be in first grade.

When he'd last seen her on the day of his college entrance ceremony, she'd still been pretty tiny.

But the girl coming through the crossing looked to be in fifth or sixth grade. The change in her appearance didn't match the flow of time.

Paying no heed to his consternation, the Mai-like girl trotted right past Sakuta. Her hair flowed out behind her, catching the corner of his eye.

"Wait!" he yelped.

He turned—

"......Huh?"

—and she was no longer there.

"......"

Were his eyes playing tricks on him? He found that hard to believe. But he didn't have time to stand here thinking about it.

——*Waiting at the reunion.*

If that message was from Ikumi, he had to go.

If she really did hurt someone, that would sure suck.

Sakuta had hoped his role would end by summoning Ikumi to Minegahara, and he had very much not planned on going an extra round.

4

Sakuta took a Kamakura-bound train from Shichirigahama Station; changed trains at Kamakura, Totsuka, and Yokohama for the Yokosuka Line, Tokaido Line, and Minatomirai Line, respectively; and finally arrived at his destination, Nihon-odori Station, after a solid hour's ride.

Out on the platform, he moved quickly toward the gates. He went so fast that after tapping his commuter pass, his legs still bumped the gates as they opened.

Following the signs, he made his way aboveground from a coastal exit. There, he broke into a run. The electronic sign at the station had told him it was now 5:51 PM.

If the invite Ikumi gave him was accurate, the reunion only ran another nine minutes.

"Why am I even doing this…?!" he gasped, trying to stifle the rising panic.

He found it hard to believe Ikumi would really hurt anyone, but he didn't have the guts to just let it be and head home. If something did happen, it would really eat at him. The knowledge that it *might* happen robbed him of all choice.

That was probably her intent.

She'd said she was waiting purely to draw him here.

He didn't know what this Ikumi was plotting. He'd been thinking about that the whole way here but found no likely answer.

Sakuta didn't get her. He felt like he'd started to get a handle on Ikumi Akagi, but that was the Ikumi who'd gone back to the other potential world. Sakuta barely knew anything about the Ikumi who actually belonged in this one. He didn't remember her.

The one thing he was sure of was that if Ikumi had gone back to the world she came from, then the Ikumi from this world had returned to it.

——*Waiting at the reunion.*

If she'd sent that message, then she must have been there.

He wasn't sure how different she was from the Ikumi he knew, so he had no clue what she could be up to. And that made him nervous.

He crossed at the walk light on the main drag. That road ran straight to the Osanbashi Pier, where luxury liners docked.

His destination was just past the intersection. A nice-looking Western building, classically styled. A very Yokohama exterior.

Sakuta caught his breath and opened the door.

As he stepped in, a voice welcomed him. There was a little chalkboard by the register that said, REUNION GUESTS TO THE ROOFTOP TERRACE. It was set up on a fancy easel.

Sakuta turned toward the stairs, but the clerk said, "That's reserved today."

Sakuta took out his invite and showed it to them.

"Oh! Go on up."

He was waved to the stairs.

The clock here showed 5:55. The reunion party would wrap up in another five. No one would expect an invitee to drop in at the last minute like this.

Second floor, third, taking his time so he could keep his breath. Only the flight to the roof itself remained. One step at a time, and he could hear the crowd ahead. Voices and laughter came drifting down.

Sensing that through the door, he turned the knob and stepped over the threshold.

The view opened up.

The restaurant stood on the shore, and the roof offered a sweeping vista. Right ahead lay the glittering lights of the liners at Osanbashi. To the left was the Red Brick Warehouse, all lit up. To the right were the lights of the Bay Bridge.

The rectangular terrace contained maybe twenty-five people. About two-thirds of his old class.

They were seated in five or six groups, talking and eating, enjoying the view.

They didn't spot Sakuta right away.

He moved toward the central buffet table, and the group seated nearest the door finally glanced his way.

Their conversation died. There was a wave of surprise and confusion…and only then did a murmur run through the room. That infected the next table over and then sparked the next.

In time, every eye in the room was on him.

"Uh, is that…?"

"Azusagawa, right?"

"Why?"

"Who invited him?"

"Don't look at me!"

He could hear whispers from all sides.

Paying that no heed, he moved to the center of the roof, eyes on the back of a girl dead ahead.

She was seated with no group, focused only on eating as much roast beef as she could. Nobody seemed to have spotted her. She was right in the middle of the room, totally out of place, and should have stood out like a sore thumb.

Sakuta wasn't distracting them—they legitimately couldn't see her.

All eyes were still on him. Some boys nearby were exchanging glances, pushing each other to be the first to speak.

But Sakuta moved right up behind *her*.

"Akagi," he said, putting his hand on her shoulder.

A ripple ran through the room. His old classmates' jaws dropped. No one managed words.

"Huh?"

"Har?"

"Uh…"

"?!"

It was all just shocked noises and gasps. Their eyes turned from Sakuta to Ikumi.

It must have looked like Ikumi appeared out of empty space.

Unable to believe the evidence of their own eyes, they started going, "What was that?" "Was Ikumi here?" "Since when?" Everyone was looking around for answers.

"I've been here for over an hour. Since before Fujino arrived late and went around tapping glasses with everyone. I was here when Tanimura knocked his glass over and it broke. And when Nakai asked Ayusawa out. The whole time."

"……"

No one said a word. Ikumi was describing real events, and that proved it. Everyone was turning pale. A wave of panic ran through the reunion venue.

Sakuta's gaze was on Ikumi's hands. She was holding a knife in her right and a fork in her left. She'd been using them to devour the roast beef. But she was still holding on to them. And they could certainly be used as weapons…

Still clutching both, she turned to face him.

"It's been a while, Azusagawa."

Her face and voice were both unmistakably Ikumi. But Sakuta could tell he didn't know *this* Ikumi. Her entire being was different. When he'd grasped her shoulder, she didn't tense up at all. His touch wasn't enough to startle her.

"You remember me?" she asked.

Even the way she talked wasn't quite like the Ikumi he knew. That Ikumi Akagi hadn't gone around testing people. Didn't have it in her.

"Totally forgot you," he said.

He'd remembered the Ikumi he met in the other world, who'd then come here from that world.

But he had almost no memories of what she'd been like in junior high. That impression wasn't being overwritten now that they were face-to-face.

"That hurts," she said, with a vague sort of smile. A deflection.

The rest of their old class were watching, riveted. Carefully judging when they should join in.

With this much attention, no one wanted to be the first to speak.

Ikumi took a long look around the terrace, then put her knife and fork together and set them down.

"Did you all see that?" she asked, addressing the crowd.

No one answered. Ikumi was relentless.

"I had Adolescence Syndrome."

She hurled a bombshell into the silence.

"No, wait, Akagi—," a male voice cried.

"Yeah, Ikumi, that's not funny!" the girl next to him chimed in.

Their words denied it, but they looked very tense. They'd *just* witnessed something unquestionably supernatural and couldn't quite refute that yet.

But he imagined this was Ikumi's goal.

Once you experienced it, you *had* to believe. There was no choice but to accept it was Adolescence Syndrome.

"Think it was a trick?" she asked flatly. "Then explain it."

Her gaze swept the room, searching for a volunteer. Not one person attempted a response. The room was now against it.

"Adolescence Syndrome exists. This is a fact."

With the roof this quiet, Ikumi didn't even need to raise her voice.

"Azusagawa wasn't wrong. We were."

"......"

Their old classmates met this claim with silence. But this one didn't last that long.

"It's a bit late to drag that up, Ikumi," the same girl said. She had a cluster of four or five girls all around her, all dressed similarly. She was clearly the group's leader. "Adolescence Syndrome? How old do you think we are?"

This was an accusation now.

If their birthday had come already, they'd be nineteen—everyone else was still eighteen. But no one bothered putting that into words.

"I'm done. That fuss Azusagawa kicked up left the teachers breathing down our necks and made our parents all lecture us, and even once we escaped to high school, this crap gets brought up every time we meet anyone from our old school. Like we're the bad guys!"

The longer she talked, the more her frustrations spilled out. And Sakuta could feel those emotions pulling the rest of the class along.

"Like, I was really worried about coming here? I never talked to any of you after graduation."

The girls around her were all nodding. The gazes of their other classmates all showed signs of agreement.

To them, this was the truth. That was how they'd all viewed the conflict at the time.

Sakuta had ruined everything. And that had followed them into high school.

"But I was glad I came! Until, like, a minute ago."

Lots of nods to that.

"I thought our third year was absolutely shit. But there were good times, too! Talking to everyone helped remind me of that."

She was now speaking for all of Class 3-1, and Ikumi was just taking that head-on. Letting all the baleful glares fall on her.

"So don't go blowing that again. Especially with that Adolescence Syndrome bullshit!"

The anger exploded.

"Yeah, Ikumi!"

"What's the point??"

The girls around her were chiming in now.

But Ikumi's expression never wavered.

"Rina, if you were so worried, why'd you come?" she asked, finally breaking her silence.

She was addressing the girl group's leader. Rina must have been her name. Even that didn't help Sakuta recall her family name. Maybe he'd never learned it. In that case, how could he remember?

"……"

Rina had no answer to Ikumi's question.

"If you were all worried, why come at all?"

Ikumi turned the question to the crowd.

Safe to assume Ikumi knew exactly why. Which was why she was asking. It was a mean question. Sakuta knew the answer himself.

"I had a dream about the reunion," someone said.

"……"

No one else spoke.

"You wrote one, too, Rina. With the dreaming hashtag."

"……"

Rina pursed her lips, stubbornly silent.

"You all did."

"……"

Still no one spoke. They couldn't admit that now. Not after rejecting the idea of Adolescence Syndrome both here and back in junior high.

Admitting it would prove their own actions weren't consistent. It would undermine the foundation of their argument. It meant admitting they were wrong and accepting their guilt. That was why they'd dug in and chose this stifling silence.

It had been just like this back in the day. The mood they'd made was crushing them.

"You remember what everyone said back then? 'Azusagawa's lost it!'"

"……"

The silence signaled agreement.

"But we're the ones who'd lost it."

"……"

"We mocked Azusagawa out of ignorance, hurt him with our false accusations, labeled him crazy, and ruined his life."

Ikumi's voice quivered. Her regrets were palpable. A mountain of shame and self-loathing lent weight to her words.

"And the way we can still laugh even though we know we're wrong proves we've lost it."

Their classmates' faces were a sea of blank slates. Like her words had paralyzed them. They were that devastating. A dangerous allure stemming from how right she was.

"B-but even so, it's a bit late!"

A boy with hair dyed brown spoke up. Every single person here likely felt the same way. But no one dared agree with him. No one even showed signs of doing so.

They'd decided that wasn't a wave to ride.

"Rina's right," Ikumi said, ignoring him, too. Her eyes were on the floor. "Because of that whole mess, not much went right for me."

"Ikumi…"

"I did *not* enjoy most of high school. It hurt to be there. That's how much I was carrying it with me."

"Then…what?" Rina asked, a hint of desperation in her voice.

"But even so, only one person has a right to put this all behind us. You, Azusagawa."

Ikumi looked up, catching his eye.

The rest of the class all turned to him.

Honestly, he was not pleased to be in the spotlight like this. Not his idea of fun. But he'd been waiting for that. For his chance to interrupt.

The sea breeze brushed by, and he took a breath.

"Noice," he said, with a goofy grin.

No one reacted. No one knew how to react yet. And their continued silence worked in his favor.

"Wow, that went even better than expected, Akagi!"

"……"

Ikumi looked just as confused.

He ignored her.

"Akagi and I go to the same college. When she told me about this reunion, I roped her into this."

"No, that's not…"

"Great trick, right? Akagi nailed the performance, too! I couldn't bring myself to stop her!"

Their classmates still weren't saying anything. Just staring fixedly at Sakuta.

"This was all a prank. I figure none of you really care, but you sure don't need to. Junior high stuff is soooo long ago."

"……"

Their faces were still frozen, like they didn't dare breathe.

"And my life was hardly ruined. I can say for a fact I am happier than *any* of you. The media kicked up a fuss, so I imagine a few of you heard? But I'm dating Mai Sakurajima. So, like…sucks to be you!"

"……"

No one spoke. Not even Ikumi.

"That was the punch line."

He'd been trying to lighten the mood, but no one seemed to think it was funny. Only Sakuta was managing an awkward smile. Most of the class seemed to think he really meant that last line.

He didn't feel like correcting that impression. This suited him just fine.

There was a part of him that felt pretty dang smug.

He hadn't planned on showing up his old classmates, but now that he had, a part of him wanted to rub it in.

So he might as well play the class black sheep till the bitter end. That had always come naturally.

"That's all I came to say."

Not like he'd ever see them again.

"I'm outta here. See ya."

He waved a hand and turned on his heel. Sakuta left the venue without anyone saying a word.

5

Outside the shop, Sakuta chose not to head directly to the nearest station.

His time in junior high had been a lot. Meeting those classmates again had definitely left him with some rough emotions. Not feeling up to going home, he spotted the Landmark Tower in the distance, and he turned right and followed the coastal road toward it.

Five minutes later, he spotted the lights of the Red Brick Warehouse on the right. Beyond that, he could see the glittering lights on the Ferris wheel, half-hidden behind the buildings.

He was headed in the direction of Sakuragicho.

Guided by the Ferris wheel lights, he passed the crowds around the warehouse. It was Sunday, and there must have been some event going on; the space outside the warehouse was still packed even after sundown.

As that hubbub retreated into the distance, the road was split by a green median strip, and he came to a giant pedestrian walkway that did a loop above four lanes of traffic. There were no pedestrian lights, so he was forced to take the overpass.

He'd imagined it was a simple circle, but once up the stairs, he soon realized it was actually an ellipse. Like a track for footraces.

Sakuta got a quarter of the way around it—and drew to a stop.

The footsteps behind him stopped, too. They'd been there for a while; he'd noticed them after passing the warehouse, but they'd likely been there since he left the party.

"Satisfied?" he asked, not turning around.

"With what?"

As expected, that was Ikumi Akagi's voice.

"Your plan went off without a hitch," he said, turning to face her.

She smiled evasively. "What plan?"

"To gather up all our junior high classmates with me watching and make them admit Adolescence Syndrome is real."

He figured that was the sole reason she'd put the reunion together. And used the dreaming hashtag to force him to be there. With a big lie about her hurting someone.

Sakuta hadn't predicted she'd use the same ruse he was using on her.

Ikumi told no lies.

He'd assumed that—or maybe she'd just tricked him into thinking that.

"You caught me," Ikumi muttered, playing along. Then she winced. "But honestly, it doesn't feel great."

"You dragged me and our old class into this scheme—you oughtta get something out of it."

Otherwise, they were all losers here.

"Yeah. If all I did was lose some friends, it's hard to laugh about."

He'd mostly been joking, but her smile was drooping pretty hard.

"How long have you been planning this?"

"Since I got Adolescence Syndrome. Figured it was the right thing to do."

That was a very Ikumi phrase. The word *right* felt like it belonged on her lips. Clearly, that was true for this world's Ikumi, too. Else that reunion incident would never have gone down that way.

"But it took me a while."

Ikumi's eyes shifted away from him, following the taillights below. A blue car took the turn and went off toward Bashamichi Station.

"When I spotted you at the college entrance ceremony…it really hit me hard."

Sakuta turned his eyes to the traffic, too.

"You were acting all normal, like nothing was wrong. Smiling like you'd forgotten all about it."

"……"

"And here I was still dragging it all around. Not making anything of myself. It was mortifying. I didn't dare face you."

"It's not like I've made anything of myself, either."

"But I felt defeated. Even though I'd been sure I was in the right…"

Sounding sad, Ikumi turned to look at him.

"……"

She seemed ready to cry, and that stole the words from him.

"You put yourself back together, Azusagawa. But I didn't make any progress. And that really hurt. I couldn't stand being there. All I wanted to do was run away."

"You got pretty far."

This world hadn't been far enough. She had to escape into another potential world.

"Not that I can criticize."

That earned him a faint smile.

"I thought I was dreaming at first."

"Yeah."

Sakuta had, too. And the Ikumi from the other side had said the same thing.

"I spent a day over there…and thought I'd be back in the morning. But I wasn't. I had to accept it was real."

"You didn't try to come back? Or want to?"

"I *was* scared."

The light below turned green. The flow of traffic went from horizonal to vertical.

"But three days passed. A week. After a full month, I started to think maybe I should just stay there."

"That world was easier for you?"

"Easier than here."

She turned a reluctant smile his way. Because he was why this world was hard for her.

"Over there, I'd flunked my college exams and was studying to try again the next year."

Like the other Ikumi said.

"So you never bumped into me at college."

"But the easiest part—our junior high stuff was already *fixed*."

"I hear I hijacked the broadcast booth and did…something."

"Mm."

The details hadn't reached him, but Kotomi Kano had told him as much while he was in that other potential world.

But the upshot was that Kaede's bullying had died out, and her Adolescence Syndrome with it. Their mother had never had her breakdown, and he'd never moved to Fujisawa with the other Kaede. They'd stayed together in the original apartment, like a normal family.

"So I figured I'd start over. Reckoned I could. In that world, I could be who I wanted to be."

"The other Akagi said the exact same thing."

Be who she wanted to be.

Or who she was trying to be.

Both Ikumis were after the same thing.

Diligent.

Righteous.

Never lying to themselves.

That's why Ikumi was here. Why she'd come back.

Ikumi Akagi was too harsh on herself to keep running.

This was how she punished herself for sins of the past.

"Azusagawa…"

"What?"

"How do I forget that I hate myself for doing nothing?"

This was likely the last thing on Earth she wanted to ask him. Ask the person who she felt had defeated her.

But she asked anyway, because she was trying to start her clock again—the clock that had stopped back in junior high.

Her eyes were filling with tears, her desperation all too evident.

"Simple."

"…Really?"

"Eat breakfast, go to school, sit in class, shoot the shit with your friends, spend time with someone you love, go to work, take a bath, brush your teeth, and go to bed. You might have some nights where you remember the bad stuff, and you're up all night, you can't breathe, and you're tossing and turning—and fall asleep somewhere along the way and wake up feeling like ass, but you eat breakfast and go to school anyway."

Sure, it would be nice if you could flip a switch and reset all the bad memories and trauma. But people didn't work like that. They didn't come with a switch that canceled out the bad times.

The only solution was to let things fade away in the flow of time. Paint things over with new memories. You'd still remember them sometimes, but even with the sleepless nights, somehow you'd face the next day with a brave face.

That's how things get forgotten.

Getting over stuff takes time.

That's how he'd become the Sakuta Azusagawa he was today.

His future progress would likely be just as inefficient.

Because he'd yet to find any other way of doing things.

"How long do I have to keep that up?"

"Beats me."

"...Fair," Ikumi whispered, staring at her feet. Then, "I really am a sad little girl."

Like she was airing out her feelings.

"Good thing you figured that out today."

"......"

"Not tomorrow, the next day, a week from now, or a year."

If she got it today, then she could start to change. This was her beginning.

"I took a long road to get here."

At last her head came up. Her eyes were on the walkway across the ellipse. If they went the other way around, they'd get there quicker, but if they kept going this way, they'd still get there in due time.

"You're right, Azusagawa."

"......Mm?"

He frowned at her.

"I'm glad it was today," she said, smiling sheepishly.

"Right?"

Sakuta returned the smile. And like that, they started walking. Clockwise around the ellipse, one step at a time.

"They all froze. Especially when you brought up your famous girlfriend."

"Isn't that what reunions are for?"

"Yours was extra mean."

"I'll thank Mai for it later."

"But you won't apologize to anyone. Very you."

"She was keeping me safe."

"......?"

Ikumi shot him a baffled look. In answer, Sakuta pulled a fashion magazine out from under his shirt.

Mai was on the cover, winking.

Last Chapter

message

The night after the reunion, an exhausted Sakuta fell asleep—and dreamed.

A highly realistic dream that felt like it was actually happening.

In the dream, he'd gone to work at his cram school and found Sara Himeji waiting for him. "I'm starting with you today, Teach!" she'd said, smiling.

Kento was delighted she'd joined his class, but Juri said not a word, not reacting at all.

Very different from your usual dreamlike chaos. Everyone in it was someone he knew. He'd taught a normal lesson and seen all three kids off at the end of it.

That was all.

But when Nasuno's paws on his face woke him up, he didn't feel like he'd escaped the dream. It had been too real.

He'd felt his body with him the whole time. He'd had thoughts running through his head. Sara's and Kento's voices still echoed in his ears.

"Was this a hashtag dreaming thing?"

He had to wonder.

"The school calendar said December first."

Sara had talked with him about what days his classes were held.

Today was Monday, November 28.

There were thirty days in November, so he'd be teaching her three days from now. Thursday.

"...Well, I'll find out when I get there."

He certainly wouldn't know beforehand.

If it was just a dream, fine.

And if it did turn out to be true, he'd have an extra student. No problem there. It would bring up his wages, so frankly, there was no downside.

He went to college like always, yawning his way through morning classes. He was still tired from the night before.

Takumi was in class with him, grumbling, "That date wear you out? Jealous." He was apparently envious of something that had only happened in his head.

"You say that, Fukuyama, but you had your hands all over Hanako's nipples."

"The Holstein from the Chiba ranch, right. Them was some beautiful teats."

He'd gone with the group from the mixer, Ryouhei, Chiharu, and Asuka. For all his griping, Takumi seemed to be making the most of college life.

At lunch, Sakuta met up with Mai in the cafeteria, and for once, no one interrupted. They were able to share a quiet meal together.

Most of the time Nodoka—or lately Miori—would join them, so this was actually fairly rare.

Having a third wheel around *did* mean they attracted a lot less attention, though.

The students here were used to seeing Mai around, but when she was with Sakuta, that was a whole other deal.

Everyone was wondering, "Why him?"

It had been much worse when they first started here.

Sakuta had ordered miso *katsu*, and Mai *shiodare* chicken. They finished eating and took a sip of tea.

"Um, Mai," he began.

"Mm?" Mai said, looking up without swallowing.

"I got something to apologize for."

She swallowed. "Cheating again?" she asked.

"When have I ever done that?"

"Every time you get to know another girl."

A swift thrust to box him in. He'd better get to the point.

"I bragged about dating Mai Sakurajima yesterday."

It had been a good way to end that interaction, but using her as a status symbol was not something he liked to do. He just didn't have a better way to prove his life wasn't ruined. She was the best proof around.

"Well, that's fine." Mai smiled. "I mean, it's true."

"Well, yeah."

"Or are you trying to say I'm not worth boasting about?"

Now she was just toying with him. She even leaned forward to peer up at him.

Naturally, he could boast about her for days.

Mai was highly boastable.

But he didn't want to make that *his* boast.

But before he could explain this…

"Mind if I join you?"

A female voice. He recognized it instantly.

He looked up and found Ikumi standing next to them.

"Please don't."

"Please do."

Sakuta and Mai spoke at once, saying literally opposite things.

"……"

Ikumi was left awkwardly standing there, unable to sit or leave.

"You're Akagi?" Mai asked. Then she urged her to sit again. "I'll go grab some tea," she added, and she grabbed Sakuta's cup and headed off to the drink bar.

If he drove Ikumi away before she got back, he would probably suffer for it.

"Fine, sit," he said.

And only then did she put her tray down across from him.

The same *shiodare* chicken Mai had ordered.

"Thanks," she said, to no one in particular. She started with her miso soup.

He figured she had a reason to come here, but it didn't seem like she was volunteering it.

So he decided to ask the question on his mind instead.

"Akagi, you sure you're better off here?"

"Why?"

"Didn't you have a boyfriend back there?"

"……Why?"

The same word, very different tone.

"Akagi was slightly prone to moans."

That was likely the source of the poltergeist he'd witnessed. The sort of sensations men and women got up to together. Feedback from the other world, flowing into this one.

"……"

Ikumi said nothing, focusing on her chicken. She didn't refute it, though, so he was probably right.

"That could be a big shock for the other Akagi. Surprise boyfriend!"

She'd not seemed experienced with those things.

"She'll be fine."

"Why?"

It was his turn to ask.

"We broke up."

"Aha."

That would solve things.

"Apparently, I'm too much."

"I get that."

"……"

That earned him a pointed glare. Perhaps he could have lied.

"And who was it?"

"Same person I was seeing here."

"Oh, him."

Seiichi Takasaka, was it? He'd only met him once and wasn't that sure of the name.

"Oh, right, you met him."

The other Ikumi must have relayed that news.

"He wants to try again."

"……"

Ikumi didn't respond. She just poker-faced her way through another piece of chicken. She had some shredded cabbage, too.

Reactions like this were not something the other Ikumi would have managed.

"I know. He called me," Ikumi said softly.

Clearly, that was her last word on the subject.

That suited him fine.

Sakuta wasn't inclined to pry further.

"So what brings you here, Akagi?"

She was at their table for a reason.

Ikumi glanced up.

Mai came back with tea.

"Should I leave?" she asked, catching the glance.

"No, this involves you."

"Does it…?"

Mai raised a brow and took a seat. She gave Sakuta a searching look, but he was equally clueless.

"Look here."

Ikumi put her soup down and showed them her palm.

——*Message from one Azusagawa to the other.*

Nice handwriting. Definitely Ikumi's.

"Akagi, is this...?"

For a moment, he thought the other Ikumi was back.

"Don't holler. I'm the one born in this world."

But the note on her palm was obviously from the other world.

"But it's not fully cured?"

"Like you said, just gotta get over it one day at a time."

"......"

He had nothing more to say about that. If Ikumi was good with it, then things likely wouldn't take a turn for the worse. He just had to hope.

"So what's the message?" Mai asked.

Ikumi pulled her hand away.

Then she put her chopsticks down and showed them her other palm.

The rest of the message.

The handwriting was sloppy, very male.

——*Find Touko Kirishima.*

——*Mai's in danger.*

This time it was in Sakuta's own handwriting.

afterword

I hope things go back to normal as soon as possible.

Hajime Kamoshida
December 2020